FULL CIRCLE

Rebecca Harrison had just become engaged to her boyfriend, Tim, and was feeling happy and content. But when she visited her brother, Damian, and his wife, Jo, she was thrown into confusion — Martin Reid was there. The last time she had seen Martin had been at Damian and Jo's wedding, three years before. On that day she had told Martin she loved him, but had been heartbroken when he rejected her. Why, when her life was at last settled, was Rebecca now beset by doubts?

Books by Margaret McDonagh
in the Linford Romance Library:

HIDDEN LOVE

MARGARET McDONAGH

FULL CIRCLE

Complete and Unabridged

LINFORD
Leicester

First published in Great Britain

First Linford Edition
published 1997

British Library CIP Data

McDonagh, Margaret
    Full circle.—Large print ed.—
    Linford romance library
    1. Love stories
    2. Large type books
    I. Title
    823.9′14 [F]

    ISBN 0–7089–5085–X

Published by
F. A. Thorpe (Publishing) Ltd.
Anstey, Leicestershire

Set by Words & Graphics Ltd.
Anstey, Leicestershire
Printed and bound in Great Britain by
T. J. Press (Padstow) Ltd., Padstow, Cornwall

This book is printed on acid-free paper

1

REBECCA HARRISON smiled to herself happily. It was a long time since her life had been so contented. The adjustments had taken three hard years, but now she was back on course, in control of her destiny. Rebecca acknowledged the fact with satisfaction and a certain amount of pride.

At twenty-one, her life was before her, and she had everything she wanted. Along with a loving family, good friends and a stable career, she now had a fiancé of — she glanced at the slim gold watch on her wrist — fifteen hours and thirty-seven minutes exactly. The solitaire ring glinted in the spring sunshine and was an unfamiliar weight on her finger. She twisted it experimentally.

Returning her attention to the road,

she approached the twin gate-posts that marked the entrance to her brother's cottage, and turned into the driveway. The gravel crunched beneath the tyres as she drew to a halt in front of the wisteria-clad façade of the whitewashed, thatched cottage.

It had been a pleasant drive down to the wilds of Dorset from her Surrey home, and she was looking forward to the surprise her arrival would bring to Damian and his wife, Jo.

Smiling, Rebecca fluffed up her dark hair and nodded encouragement to her reflection in the driver's mirror.

"The past is in the past, where it belongs," she told herself, her voice strong with determination.

She collected her overnight bag from the back seat and went to the front door where she gave the old horseshoe knocker a firm but jaunty rap. Damian opened the door, and before he could speak, she threw herself into his arms and was enveloped in a bear-like embrace.

"Rebecca!"

"It's so wonderful to see you!"

Eight years her senior, her brother had been her rock, her anchor in troubled waters, first when their parents had died in a flying accident, and more recently in the last difficult years. Damian was always there for her and she loved him to bits.

"What are you doing here?" he exclaimed as he released her and stepped back a pace. "I thought you were too busy to come down for weeks."

She grinned impishly. "I had a change of plans. Besides, I'm never too busy for you, and it is your wedding anniversary. I come bearing gifts." Rebecca sobered as she glanced at her brother's face, disconcerted by the slight frown that drew his dark brows together. "Have I put my foot in it? Are you and Jo planning something romantic?" Anxiety brought a huskiness to her voice.

"No, no, it's not that — " Damian

3

smiled and drew her indoors. "You just surprised me, that's all. Anyway, I'm on call over the week-end so we hadn't planned to go out. Come on through. You're just in time for food, as usual!"

Reassured of her welcome, Rebecca laughed and followed him to the kitchen where Jo was tossing a salad. More sister than sister-in-law, Jo's marriage to her brother had not upset their closeness as Rebecca had once feared. Instead, she had added a wonderful new dimension to their small family.

"You look positively glowing," Jo greeted her with a warm hug. "Why didn't you let us know you were coming?"

"Spur of the moment decision. I hope it isn't inconvenient?"

"Of course not, it's wonderful to see you. It's just that we — well, we — " Jo broke off and glanced at her husband for help.

Damian's brows knitted together in

4

another frown. "We have someone staying for a few days, that's all. There's plenty of room though."

"Why don't you go upstairs and freshen up?" Jo suggested. "Lunch will be ready in about five minutes."

Rebecca went upstairs to the lilac-hued spare room and sighed in contentment at the view of the glorious countryside beyond the window. It looked fresh and green, the air full of scents and the sound of the varied local bird population. It was no wonder Damian and Jo had settled so happily here, she thought with a twinge of envy.

After a hasty freshen up, she returned downstairs to join the others for lunch. As she walked along the hall, she heard voices in the sitting-room and her steps faltered. Rebecca shook her head. No, she must have been mistaken, but just for a moment she thought . . . It couldn't be, but one of the voices had sounded painfully familiar.

A lump formed in her throat as she

forced herself to enter the room. Her gaze slid past Damian and Jo and came to rest on the other occupant of the room. He was standing by the window, the sunlight behind him making it difficult for her to see his face, but with dread and panic, she knew she had not made a mistake. Martin Reid was unmistakable.

Faded jeans encased his long, lean legs, and his black sweatshirt added to his dark and almost sinister appearance. His hair was cut shorter than she remembered, but was just as ebony, thick and rakish as ever. And the eyes. Although they were shadowed, she knew that under the straight, black brows, they would be watchful and intense, the colour changing from midnight blue to steel grey with his mood.

That he inspected her as thoroughly, Rebecca had no doubt. She could feel the effect of his gaze upon her and a knot of tension formed in the pit of her stomach.

"Hello, Becky."

As he stepped towards her, she moved away, maintaining the distance between them. The husky timbre of his voice sent a shiver of awareness down her spine. His sensuous mouth, that promised so much, curved in a half smile as she licked her dry lips and cleared her throat.

"Martin. I didn't k-know you were h-here," she stammered, furious that the very sight of him had the power to rob her of her self-control.

His dark lashes flicked up and she was subjected to the full force of his gaze. He regarded her in silence, and with every second that passed, Rebecca felt electricity charge the air.

When Jo rose to her feet and announced that lunch was ready, Rebecca sighed with relief and gratitude. She needed a moment to pull herself together. The shock of Martin's presence had rocked her to the core. Just when she had been so happy and contented and positive her life had taken a turn for the better, fate had intervened. Later there would be time to analyse her thoughts. For the time being, she had to act normally and pretend that seeing Martin again meant nothing to her.

It was difficult to present an unconcerned façade when she sat a short distance from Martin on the other side of the pine table. Each time she glanced up, it was to find his gaze upon her, the expression in his eyes unfathomable. Her appetite had deserted her, and she thought each mouthful would choke her.

"What's that on your finger?"

Martin's voice snapped her from her reverie, and she set down her knife and fork with studied care. Three gazes rested on her.

"That was part of my surprise." She smiled tremulously at Damian. "I wanted to tell you in person. Last night Tim asked me to marry him and I said yes."

She saw Martin's eyes turn from blue to glint steel grey and swallowed down a wave of apprehension. It was none of his business. Whatever he thought was no concern of hers.

"I'm very happy for you." Jo smiled and squeezed her arm. "You never hinted this was in the wind!"

"We've been going out together for some time. It can't be that much of a surprise."

Damian leaned across and kissed her cheek. "So long as you are happy, that's all that matters."

"When is the wedding?" Martin asked with a brief lift of an eyebrow.

Rebecca gritted her teeth and forced a smile. "We've not set a date yet, but probably in the autumn."

"Don't forget to send me an invitation," Martin said.

"If I thought you would come — "

"Becky, I wouldn't miss it for anything," he mocked softly and raised his glass in a brief toast.

She returned her attention to her plate to evade his probing gaze. To her relief, Damian claimed his interest, and while they talked, she cast several secretive glances at Martin. He had changed in the three years since she had seen him. His face was thinner, more harshly angled than before, the strong jawline more prominent in a way that only served to give him a more masculine attractiveness. And heaven knew, he had always been far too good looking for any woman's peace of mind.

He also appeared to be more distant, more reticent, and she detected, too, an air of cynicism, as if he had seen too much, done too much. She wondered where he had been and what he had been doing in the last three years.

Rebecca reined in her thoughts in disgust. Her days of allowing Martin to invade her every thought and dream were long gone. He was nothing to her now. She had to believe that, or all she had worked through meant nothing.

When lunch was over, she helped with the dishes, then followed Damian through to the sitting-room. She declined coffee, and sat back in a deep, chintz-covered armchair and listened half-heartedly as Damian recounted an amusing incident with a patient. A dull pain began to throb behind her eyes and across her forehead. Unconsciously, she massaged her temples with her fingers.

The headaches had been better lately — fewer and further between. She hoped she was not too optimistic in her belief they would eventually stop altogether, but had to remember it was a long process on the road to recovery.

"Rebecca?"

Her brother's voice impinged on her consciousness and she focused her disturbed gaze on his face. "Mmm?"

"Are you all right?" he queried softly with both brotherly and doctorly concern.

"I'm fine," she assured, aware that Martin's gaze rested on her. "Just a bit of a headache. If you don't mind, I think I'll go and lie down for a while."

Damian followed her to the foot of the stairs. "Is there anything I can do for you?"

"No, I have my pills if I need them. Don't worry, Damian. They are getting better."

He kissed her forehead and smiled. "Try and have a sleep."

In her room, Rebecca had a sip of water, then lay down on the bed and closed her eyes. But there was no relief from Martin's image. Only that morning she had been so confident that she had at last come out of a dark tunnel into the light. Now it was as though the three years of struggle had been undone.

She turned on to her side as if turning her back on him. Martin, her brother's best friend, her mystery man. He had floated in and out of her childhood, a shadowy figure in her growing-up years. He had been special, exciting, and he had left a deep impression on her. She had become infatuated with him, she admitted, besotted, her teenage, romantic mind filled with increasingly exotic dreams of how he would love her, of their happy-ever-after life together.

She had nearly allowed him to ruin her life . . . had nearly lost her life because of her misery and infatuation with him, and he didn't even know it. Martin didn't care about her. She had accepted the fact, but it had been a painful and humiliating lesson to learn.

That their paths would cross again eventually had always been a worry, but as the months had drifted into years, so her anxiety had lessened. Now, seeing him again, unprepared, had brought all the pain and torment back.

Sleep claimed her, and when she woke just after three thirty, she was thankful that the headache had not developed. She left the bed, soaked a flannel with cool water and held it to her face. In the mirror, she could see that her face was pale, that her eyes had dulled with anxiety.

Rebecca went to sit on the narrow

window seat and looked out across the garden to the fields and woods beyond. She clasped her knees to her chest and watched two starlings chase each other over a morsel of food.

When the bedroom door opened, she turned, disconcerted when Martin stepped into the room. She sucked in a breath, dragged her gaze from his, and returned her attention to the garden.

"Have you never heard of knocking?" she asked with a flash of sarcasm.

"I thought you might be asleep." He walked across the room and stood near her. "Are you feeling better?"

"Yes, thank you."

"I brought you some tea."

Surprised, she looked round and offered a smile as she accepted the cup he held out for her. "Thanks."

She sipped the strong brew, and an uncomfortable silence stretched between them. She wished he would go, wished he had never come back into her life.

Disconcerted by his nearness, Rebecca

swung her legs to the floor and moved away from him. Did the force of his masculine presence, his looks, affect every woman he met? An ironic smile pulled at her mouth. Perhaps she was allergic to him as his very presence in the same room caused an adverse reaction.

Martin thrust his hands into the pockets of his jeans and studied her. "It's been a long time."

"Three years. Damian and Jo's wedding, to be precise," she riposted, her chin raised in challenge.

She fought back the flood of memories of the last time she had seen him. To remember made her ashamed of her own behaviour and angry at the hurt he had caused, the smart of humiliation and embarrassment.

As he took a step towards her, his eyes narrowed, she circled away from him, regretting her challenge, this cat and mouse game between them.

"If you'll excuse me, I'll go and help Jo downstairs."

Martin caught her arm before she reached the door. "No you won't. Firstly, Jo has gone to town to fetch something, and Damian has been called out to a patient. Secondly, you and I have not finished our chat."

"I think we have." She was disconcerted that they were alone in the house. "Let me go. I need some fresh air."

"Then we'll go for a walk."

"No! I want to be alone," she insisted and tried to free her arm from his hold.

"Three years ago you would have welcomed my company."

Rebecca sucked in an angry breath at his taunt. "I'm older and wiser now."

His eyes darkened to grey as she flung the word at him. "Becky — "

"Don't call me that," she berated him. She hated it because he was the only one who used it, and it reminded her too much of him and the past. "There is nothing for us to talk about."

"We have three years to catch up on."

"I think not."

He paused for a moment and held her gaze. "Don't you want to know what I've been doing?"

"I can imagine. Same old Martin, moving here, moving there, a girl in every port. Well, I'm not interested in your disappearing acts, or your little secrets. You've drifted in and out of my life for as long as I can remember. Once I wanted to unravel the mysteries of your existence. Now I don't care any more."

Shutters dropped down to hide the expression in his eyes, and it was as though he had physically withdrawn from her. He dropped her arm as if the touch of her disgusted him, and Rebecca stepped back, alarmed at the anger she sensed in him.

His gaze slid over her in brief assessment before he turned away. At the door, he turned and raised a hand in mocking salute. "Enjoy your walk."

17

Rebecca did not enjoy her walk. The paths usually brought her joy and peace. Now, her mind was in turmoil, the peace she craved denied her.

She had rebuilt a good life, and would not allow Martin to spoil it all, would refuse to allow him to make her life a misery. She felt a flash of uncharacteristic annoyance at Damian. He had made no mention that Martin was back, that he had seen him, but then why should he? Martin's name had not been mentioned between them for three years. Not for the first time, she wondered just how much her brother knew about her behaviour on the day of the wedding, of the scene with Martin.

The memory of it brought a fresh wave of shame . . .

2

AT nine o'clock on the morning of the wedding, Martin had not arrived. Neither the groom nor the bride appeared worried, but as the minutes ticked by, Rebecca's anxiety grew.

"This is just typical of him," she complained to her brother in a mixture of genuine concern and personal disappointment. "He's so unreliable."

"He's not unreliable," Damian defended with amused calm.

"How can you say that? This is the most important day of your life. Martin is supposed to be your best man, and not only has he failed to arrive, neither has he phoned! If that isn't unreliable, it is plain inconsiderate."

"Go back and help Jo," Damian said. "You're making me nervous."

"But — "

"Rebecca, he'll be here. Now go and put on that knockout dress. I'm sure Martin will notice!"

Rebecca's cheeks flushed scarlet at her brother's teasing. No doubt Damian thought it funny that his little sister blushed in the presence of his mysterious, exciting best friend, but she was not amused. Her feelings for Martin were not girlish infatuation — she loved him. He was so different from the boys she knew, all of them boring and immature. And none of the ones she had kissed had generated the excitement of the one she had stolen from Martin under the mistletoe the Christmas of her sixteenth year.

Today, with her new hairstyle and the exquisite bridesmaid's dress, she would show Martin that she was not sixteen any more. She would prove to everyone she could be just as sophisticated and desirable as the next woman.

As she bathed and dressed in the plush environs of Jo's family home in Gloucestershire, Rebecca endeavoured to push Martin from her mind. In the flurry of activity in the last moments before the ceremony, this proved easier than she had imagined. Before she knew it, they were at the village church, and as she entered, her gaze was drawn to the alter rail. There was Damian, flushed with happiness, and yes, Martin had arrived.

Her heart contracted at the sight of him. He looked wonderful, and the formality of his morning suit failed to tame the air of wildness and rakish excitement that never ceased to make her pulse race.

When Martin met her gaze, all her nerve endings prickled in awareness. His gaze travelled leisurely over her from head to toe and back again, his eyes intent with surprise and . . . what? Admiration? A renewed rush of excitement and hope swept through her. She hoped he would see her as a woman, not his best friend's little sister.

As she concentrated on the beautiful

service, she wished her parents could have been present. Their permanent loss was an upset that remained with her, but especially this day when they would have been so happy and proud of Damian.

When the formalities were over, the photographs completed, they moved on to the reception at the village hall. The meal was sumptuous, and so was the champagne. Rebecca drank more of it than she should, but she needed the Dutch courage. When the dancing began, emboldened by the wine, she made her way to Martin's side.

"We're meant to dance together . . . it's traditional."

He looked down at her, his eyes very blue. "Then let's go — if you're sure you don't mind dancing a slower one with an old man like me."

"You're not old," Rebecca protested, taking his hand and urging him to the dance floor.

Beneath the teasing in his voice, she noted the hint of warning but was determined to ignore it. The eight-year gap between them did not matter, not if they cared for each other. And she would make Martin love her. She slipped her arms around his neck and moved close to him, piqued when he smiled down at her, removed her hands from him and held her father away.

"Behave yourself, Becky," he told her as he steered her round the floor. "And go easy on the champagne."

Furious that he was treating her as though she were still a child, her voice held an uncharacteristic snap. "You aren't my keeper. If I want some more champagne, I shall have it."

"Suit yourself." He shrugged. "Just don't come running to me if you make an idiot of yourself."

"I won't. I'm grown up now, and you don't have to pretend you are some kind of substitute father."

Martin's eyes glinted steel grey and his lips thinned to an angry line. "I think we've danced enough to satisfy tradition, don't you?"

He led her from the dance floor and walked away, his tall figure soon lost in the crowded room. Rebecca stared after him, overwhelmed by bitter disappointment. Things were not working out as she had planned. After the wedding, Martin was to take her home, and she had been looking forward to the time alone with him. Now he was angry with her, and she was afraid their time together would be spoiled.

Later in the afternoon, she saw Martin watching her from across the room. She raised her glass to him in salute and downed the contents too quickly, giggling as the bubbles tickled her nose. Martin frowned at her and turned away.

When Damian and Jo finally left, Rebecca returned to the house with Jo's parents and prepared to leave. She changed into a loose-flowing dress, leaving her hair in its sophisticated style. Then she packed her bags and went downstairs to wait for Martin and say her goodbyes to Jo's parents.

As she entered the sitting-room, her gaze locked with Martin's and her pulse raced. He looked masculine and exciting in his jeans and his blue-grey shirt that emphasised the extraordinary colour of his eyes.

"I've just made some tea. You will have some before you leave?" Jo's mother invited.

"Thanks, Mrs Miller." Martin smiled. "I'd love some."

Rebecca nodded her agreement and sat down on the settee, peculiarly glad to put off the moment when she would be alone with Martin. Time with him was what she had wanted, and yet now, she was nervous.

After their tea, Martin suggested they be on their way, and having thanked the Millers for their hospitality, they were soon in the car and heading towards the motorway. Silence stretched between them, and Rebecca was tense, determined she should not waste the opportunity yet anxious how best to carry out her plans.

Martin appeared to be in a relaxed mood, despite their disagreement at the reception. Although she had known him most of her life, she knew very little of his life, what he did, the things that mattered to him. He had always been wary of talking about himself, and his very mysteriousness had added to his appeal, the excitement she felt. Boldened by her new resolve, she cast him a sideways glance.

"I wasn't sure if you would come today. You were awfully late."

"I'm sure Damian knew I wouldn't let him down."

Rebecca cleared her throat. "He said that you'd been abroad again recently?"

"That's right."

"What doing?"

"Nothing much."

"But where did you go?" Rebecca tried to hide her frustration. She was making no headway at all. "What sort of work is it that you do exactly?"

"I've told you before."

"No, you haven't," she countered, cross at his calmness. "You just muttered about the Civil Service or something."

Martin glanced at her and smiled. "There you are then."

"But you must do something!"

"As little as possible."

"So why go abroad then?"

"To do as little as possible in warmer and more exotic places!"

Rebecca frowned her annoyance. "I don't believe you. Why won't you tell me? What's the big secret?"

"Why this sudden interest in my affairs?" he asked, his voice more cautious.

"I'm only trying to make conversation — "

"Oh, is that what it is?" He laughed. "I thought it was more like an inquisition!"

"You ask questions about me, and I don't act so secretively," she snapped at him, annoyed he was making fun of her. "But then, I've got nothing to hide."

Martin threw her a speculative glance, his eyes slate grey. "What makes you think I have anything to hide?"

"I just meant — "

"Perhaps there is nothing to tell. Perhaps you are more interesting than me."

With a sigh, Rebecca turned to stare sightlessly from the window. It was like trying to get blood from a stone, she thought crossly.

"Cat got your tongue, sweetheart?" Martin teased.

She glared at his smiling profile. "I give up."

"Good idea!"

"I wasn't that interested, anyway," she lied, stung by his amusement.

He raised an eyebrow, his smile widening. "Of course not!"

Rebecca lapsed into silence for a while to soothe her ruffled feathers. He really was the most infuriating, intriguing man she had ever met! After a few moments, she glanced across at him again.

"Will you tell me about Devon? I've never been, and you used to have a farm there, didn't you? Is that safe enough?" she added. "Or am I being too inquisitive?"

"Sarcasm doesn't become you." He smiled, and paused for a moment as the traffic slowed to negotiate a contraflow system. "I still have the farm. It belonged to my parents. I grew up there."

"What was it like?"

"Very isolated. We lived a typical country life, I guess. It was a wonderful way to spend a childhood, and I've had a deep love of the countryside and farming ever since."

"Do you go there much?" she asked, fascinated by this side of his character and the information he was sharing about himself for the first time.

"When I can. The house is in good shape, and I let the land to a neighbouring farmer."

"Will you go back there?"

"One day," he told her, an almost wistful tone in his voice. "Yes, one day I'll settle down there, do some farming, breed horses maybe — "

Rebecca swallowed. She had never thought of Martin in this way before, never imagined his roots, considered his dreams. His parents were dead, she knew, and he had no living relatives. Clearly his childhood had been a happy one, and she wondered what had made him leave.

"Martin, if you want to farm, why didn't you stay in Devon?"

He was quiet for so long, she thought he would not answer, but when he finally spoke, his voice held a tinge of remembered sadness.

"I was twelve when my mother died. Looking back, I realise she had never been well, but I was too young to see it, or too selfish."

As he paused for a moment, lost in his private thoughts, Rebecca studied his profile and noted the sombre expression in his blue-grey eyes when he glanced across at her.

"After she died," he continued, "Dad gave up — he had no will to live. His sister came to look after us, but Dad withdrew into himself and gradually the place fell into disrepair. I was so used to doing everything with him, I couldn't understand why he wouldn't pay any attention to me. Anyway, after about six months, he went up to bed one night and never woke up."

"I'm sorry."

"If it was possible, I'd say he died of a broken heart. He just loved my mother too much."

Rebecca clasped her hands together in her lap to resist the impulse she had to reach out to him. "What happened then?"

"My aunt took me back to her house in London, and there I stayed, hating every minute of it, making us both miserable, probably. She sent me off on an adventure holiday one summer. That's where I met Damian."

"I never knew that!"

Martin smiled. "You were about six, I think. Quite the little heartbreaker, too, as I remember!"

"And the farm?" Rebecca asked, cursing the heat that stained her cheeks.

"It was closed up for a long time." Martin sighed. "I managed to hang on to it, but there was never any money to put it back in order. I had to do something else to fund the plans I had for it. It's just taken longer than I anticipated."

"What about your aunt?"

"I'm afraid she died a few years ago. She was good to me, and I'm grateful, but we were never close."

Rebecca was moved by what he had told her. He was always so controlled, so tough almost, that to see him vulnerable tore at her heart. It must have been an ordeal for a young boy to lose both his parents within six months, for a world that had been happy and secure to change so radically.

"It must have been horrible for you," she told him, a huskiness in her voice.

Martin reached out and touched her hand. "Becky, I'm sorry. I didn't mean to make you think about your parents."

"That's all right. I've been thinking about them a lot today, with the wedding and everything."

"It must have been a strange day for you," he sympathised. "Pleased and sad at the same time."

She nodded, surprised at his perception. "I'm so happy for Damian, and I love Jo. It's just that it's been only Damian and me for nearly three years and I feel . . . " She paused, uncertain.

"Deserted?"

"Yes, in a way. That must sound silly."

"No, it doesn't. It's understandable. Damian has been the most important person in your life recently, and it is natural you should feel a little confused and alone at such a big change."

"I didn't think anyone would

understand," she admitted. "I didn't want to seem selfish. I know Damian will always be there for me, and now there's Jo as well, but you're right, I did feel a bit alone."

"You'll be all right, you'll see," Martin said with such assurance that she smiled back at him.

As dusk darkened the sky around them, Rebecca yawned and relaxed back in the seat. She thought again of the boy Martin had been, of what it must have been like for him to see first his mother and then his father slip away.

His words about his father's love for his mother plagued her. Was that why he appeared to have a string of girlfriends, why she had once heard him tell Damian he had no intention of settling down for years? Was he afraid to love anyone too deeply because of what he thought love had done to his father?

Rebecca bit her lip and looked at his profile as he concentrated on his driving and they left the motorway and turned on to the quieter, rural roads of Surrey.

"Martin?"

"Mmm?"

"Do you really think you can love someone too much?"

He glanced at her, his expression guarded. "How do you mean?"

"I think the love and happiness your parents shared far outweighed your father's period of unhappiness. I loved my parents, and miss them deeply, but I am glad of the time we did have together. I'm sure your father would not have given up one minute of his time with your mother for worry about what may happen when she was gone.

"I know this isn't my business, but none of what happened was your fault, nor does it mean that your father didn't love you. You can't let your feelings as a child colour the rest of your life in case something happens to you as it did to your father."

As the silence lengthened between

them, she was terrified she had been too outspoken, too forceful in her desire to express her concern and her compassion. A flutter of alarm assailed her as Martin pulled the car off the road and into a lay-by.

He turned to look at her, and she was mesmerised by the intensity of his deep-blue gaze. In slow motion, it appeared to her, he reached out a hand towards her face, and trailed one firm finger down her cheek. Her skin burned from his touch. She unconsciously licked her lips and saw his gaze move to her mouth. For one insane, wonderful moment, she thought he would kiss her, willed him to, but after an interminable time, he drew back from her.

"You are very wise for one so young."

His withdrawal and his words brought a rush of bitter disappointment. She closed her eyes to hide her emotions as he eased the car into gear and pulled back on to the road. Had she imagined he had so nearly kissed her? She could still feel the touch of his finger on her skin, wanted to relive every instant again, but Martin's voice, controlled and impersonal, cut into her thoughts.

"Now your exams are over, you'll be doing Psychology, I guess?"

"Yes," she replied, attempting to match his tone. "If I've passed."

"You will."

"I wish I could be that certain."

"You're intelligent, you've worked hard, and psychology is what you've always wanted to do, right?" he persisted, and she nodded in agreement. "That's it then."

"I wish it was that easy!" She laughed, pleased the tension between them since the incident in the lay-by had relaxed. "I still have to hope I'm accepted at university — then I have to pass all that."

Martin made no further comment as he turned the car into the drive of the mellow brick house awash with Virginia Creeper that she had lived in all her life.

"Here we are then," he said as he switched off the engine and turned to look at her. "You'll miss the house when you're at university."

"It will be a wrench leaving, even if it is only temporary," she agreed with a glance at the darkened bulk of the house. Rebecca looked back at him, desperate not to let him leave, and she tried to hide the desire in her eyes as he returned her gaze. "You'll come in for a while?"

She held her breath as he hesitated. Her heart slammed against her ribs, and her fingers knotted together with anxiety in her lap.

"All right," he allowed at last. "Just for a few minutes."

Relieved, Rebecca left the car and opened the front door, dropping her case in the hall. Her spirits soared. Martin's presence filled the house and she hugged the knowledge that for the time being, she had him to herself. What she made of that time was up to her.

She drew the sitting-room curtains and switched on the table lamps, the apricot hue of the decor casting a warm glow to the room. Martin sat on the settee, his long legs stretched out in front of him.

"Would you like something to drink?" she asked, mortified that her voice quivered with sudden nerves.

"Coffee would be nice, thanks."

She could feel his gaze on her as she went to the kitchen. Now he was here, with her, alone, tension and excitement wound her nerves into knots. She took several deep breaths to calm herself as she made the coffee and put some biscuits on a plate.

When she returned to the sitting-room, the sight of Martin, casual and relaxed, threatened to destroy the self-control she had mustered. She handed Martin a mug of coffee and hovered anxiously.

"Sit down, Becky," Martin told her after a moment of awkward silence. "Stop trying so hard."

Self-conscious, she sat on the edge of the settee next to him and nervously picked at the constraining knot that held her hair in its sophisticated style. When Martin lazily reached out and pulled the pins free, she started, and her curls tumbled down around her face and shoulders.

"That's better." He smiled.

"Why? What was wrong with it?"

"It suits you better this way."

"I thought it made me look . . . older."

Martin held her gaze, his expression sombre. "Becky, don't try to be something you're not."

Her hands clenched to fists, her nails carving half-moon crescents in her palms. This was not working how she intended. Martin was supposed to realise she was a woman, not keep reminding her of the child she had been. Why wouldn't he see she was not a little girl any more?

Martin set down his mug and looked at his watch. "I'd better be going," he said, confirming her worst fears.

She had to find a way to delay his departure. Meeting his gaze boldly, she edged closer to him. His eyes narrowed and turned greyer as he looked at her, and although her heart had begun to beat a rapid tattoo, her voice remained steady.

"You could always stay."

His eyes regarded her for a moment, an eyebrow raised at her invitation.

"No, I couldn't."

"Why not?"

"Because it wouldn't be a good idea — for either of us." His eyes hooded to hide his expression, and he ran the fingers of one hand through the rakish thickness of his dark hair.

As Rebecca watched him, her fingers ached to follow the path of his. She leaned towards him and placed a hand on his chest. "I — "

"Becky," he warned sternly, his hands on her arms to hold her away.

Undaunted, she bent towards him and kissed him boldly on the mouth. He jerked her away from him, and she saw a pulse beat along the line of his jaw.

"Stop it."

"Don't you like me?"

"That has nothing to do with it. Becky, I — "

"Please," she whispered against his mouth in provocation. He raised a hand to her face to hold her from him, but his fingers slid on into her hair and clenched in the silky thickness. Rebecca sucked in a breath. "Please, kiss me."

As she touched her lips to his once more, he swore under his breath, and then his mouth opened hotly on hers. Her hands slid around his neck, and she murmured involuntarily at the sweetness of his kiss, unprepared for the intensity of the emotions that threatened to overwhelm her.

The blood rushed through her veins. Just as she instinctively pressed herself closer to him, needing him to ease the ache that burned inside her, he dragged his mouth from hers.

"Martin?"

"This is crazy," he muttered harshly.

Terrified of his withdrawal, she clung to him. "Martin, please."

"No!"

He rose to his feet and dumped her unceremoniously on the settee. Rebecca stared up at him in confusion, tears in her eyes as she stretched out a hand to him in appeal.

"Martin — "

"It shouldn't have happened."

"Why not?" she demanded desperately. "I love you, I — "

"No, you do not, Rebecca," he interrupted. "Look at you. You have no idea what you're doing."

A tear slipped from the corner of her eye and she brushed it away angrily. "I do know. I want you to love me."

"I can't. You're too young."

The coldness in her voice chilled her soul. "I'll do anything you want," she pleaded.

"Don't make things any worse."

Martin evaded her and moved away. His rejection was painful, the hurt like a lance through her heart. He could not do this to her, could not be so cruel.

"I suppose there's another woman," she accused jealously.

"That is none of your business."

"But is that the reason?"

"No."

"Then why?"

Martin sighed and dragged his fingers through his hair. His expression was stony, his voice hard, distant, as cutting as the look in his angry grey eyes.

"There can be nothing between us, Rebecca. I like my women to be women, not inexperienced, young girls. I don't need you," he finished, his gaze level and determined.

Rebecca stared at him in shock. "You're just going to leave?"

"That's right."

"Then go!" she shouted as tears fell unchecked at his harsh and painful words. "I hate you, do you hear me? I never want to see you again as long as I live!"

"When you understand, we'll talk

44

about it," he told her quietly.

"Hell will freeze over first."

For a moment he watched her, his expression unreadable, then he turned and walked across the room. At the door, he turned and hesitated but he did not look at her. "You'll thank me one day."

"Never!"

Rebecca heard the front door close, and shortly afterwards his car engine fired to life before he reversed out of the drive and pulled away with a squeal of tyres on Tarmac.

As the sound of the car died away, Rebecca sank to her knees in the middle of the sitting-room floor, and cried as she had not cried for a long time.

3

"AND now Martin is back," Rebecca murmured aloud as she snapped free of her painful reverie.

She leaned against a lichen-covered fence and stared at a flock of sheep in the adjoining field. They stared back, their eyes wary as they watched her.

"I know," she told them. "I'm crazy, right?"

Several bleated in apparent agreement then returned to the task of munching the lush spring grass. Rebecca shook her head and turned to retrace her footsteps back to the cottage. There was still dinner to be endured, but she had decided to leave soon afterwards. She would not spend a night under the same roof as Martin.

Three years was a long time, but she could still recall the bitterness and hurt . . . and her shame at her foolish behaviour. There had been no reason to assume Martin was interested in her in any other way than his best friend's sister. But she had brazenly attempted to seduce him, and whilst she had brought his rejection upon herself, it was no less painful for that.

Had he known all the time what she was trying to do? Had it amused him? He had played with her emotions in the cruellest way, and it had taken longer than he knew for her to recover from the after-effects.

The morning after the scene with Martin, she had wandered around in a daze of misery. She found herself at the cemetery, and stood at the foot of her parents' graves, overwhelmed by their loss, feeling apart from Damian, saddened and confused about Martin. As she left the cemetery, her mind in a whirl of torment, she had stepped out into the road without conscious thought. Vaguely, she had heard someone shout, had hesitated in mid-stride, turned, seen the bus, and then . . .

"Rebecca!"

The sound of her brother calling her name intruded on her painful memories. She looked up and forced a smile as he walked across the garden and met her at the gate.

"You've been gone for ages. Are you all right?"

"I'm fine. I'm sorry if you were worried. I was enjoying the fresh air."

As she walked back to the cottage with him, she wondered just what he knew of past events. Had Martin said anything to him? She herself had simply said that they had argued, that she did not want to talk about it. By the time she left hospital and her long convalescence had begun, Damian appeared to have forgotten all about the problem between Martin and herself, and his name had never been mentioned. Rebecca had hoped it would stay that way.

She had hated Martin with every

fibre of her being. She hated him for the humiliation he had meted out, for the cruel end to all her dreams, for walking out on her without a backward glance. Despite everything that had happened, a longing for him sometimes caught her unawares . . . and for that she hated him most of all.

"I found her," Damian announced as he ushered her into the sitting-room to join Jo and Martin.

Rebecca bit down a flash of irritation at the fuss they had made — as if she were still a child! She was intensely aware of Martin's presence, but she forced herself not to meet his gaze. When Jo refused her offer to help with dinner and disappeared to the kitchen, Rebecca wished she could find a plausible excuse to leave the room, but she did not wish to give Martin the satisfaction of knowing he made her uncomfortable.

When Damian was called to the telephone, she sat tense and wary as she became the object of Martin's regard.

"What are you doing with yourself these days?" he asked.

"Working. You?" she queried with polite formality.

"I'm back on the farm now, getting it back into shape. I'm starting to breed horses."

Rebecca swallowed a sudden restriction in her throat. "That's nice."

"Becky," Martin snapped with annoyance. "Can't we talk like civilised human beings?"

"I'm sorry, I thought we were."

His gaze captured hers, and despite her desire to look away, she refused to back down. The blue-grey eyes watched her with lazy speculation.

"Tell me about your intended."

"Why?" she asked warily as his lashes slipped down to hide his expression. "What do you want to know?"

"What's his name? Where did you meet? What does he do?"

"If you'll give me a few moments, I'll write up a dossier on him for you to study."

50

Martin raised his brows at the sarcasm in her tone, and she rued her error in allowing him to bait her. Now she had roused his infernal curiosity, and once he took the bit between his teeth, he could be stubbornly persistent.

"His name is Tim Stevens. He's an accountant, and I met him at work," she told him with reluctance. "Satisfied?"

"No. What has an accountant got to do with psychology?"

Damn him! She would have to be more careful. "I work for a group of accountants," she said through gritted teeth.

"But your psychology! I thought you would pass with flying colours."

"No."

"Why not?"

"Because I didn't take it."

Martin leaned towards her and rested his elbows on his knees. His eyes darkened disturbingly. "But psychology was the only thing you ever wanted to do. You were so adamant — "

"Well, I changed my mind," she interrupted crossly. She was not going to tell him about the accident, the long months of recuperation, her period of depression, her disappointment at the shattering of her dreams. She would not tell him she had taken the job at the accountants for much needed money, nor that she was struggling in her spare time to study for her degree.

"What happened?" he probed.

He stood up and moved towards her. Alarmed, she, too, rose to her feet and put the sturdy couch between them.

"Nothing," she lied. "I just decided to do something else. Is that so surprising?"

"To me it is. I think there is more you're not telling me."

"Do you? Well, my life is no concern of yours, and there is no point in this ridiculous conversation!"

Before he could respond, Damian came back into the room, and Rebecca made her excuses and went upstairs to change before dinner. When she looked in the mirror above the vanity basin, her face was flushed, her eyes haunted. She splashed some cold water on her face and applied a light make-up.

She would do her utmost to keep the animosity between herself and Martin hidden in front of Damian and Jo. She had no wish to give them further cause to wonder at the distance that had grown between the best man and bridesmaid since the wedding. And for their sakes, as this was to be a happy occasion, she vowed to keep a check on her temper and not allow Martin to raise her ire.

The meal was delicious, and Rebecca found that her appetite had returned. It appeared Martin had reached similar conclusions to her own, as he did nothing to spoil the friendly atmosphere that bubbled around the dinner table, but he did watch her. She could feel his gaze resting on her like a physical touch.

After dinner, they had coffee in the sitting-room. Rebecca chose a comfortable armchair away from Martin and out of the direct line of his gaze. She would have to turn her head to look at him, and that she was determined not to do.

She realised with regret that any suggestion that she leave that evening would bring too many questions. She had no desire to draw attention to her discomfort with Martin. However, when Damian and Jo decided to retire, she jumped to her feet, unwilling to be left alone in Martin's company.

"Is it all right if I use the phone?" she asked as Damian hugged her goodnight.

"Of course. Help yourself."

"Thanks."

She went to use the wall phone in the kitchen and deliberately closed the door. She did not want Martin to overhear her conversation and she hoped he would have gone to bed by the time she had finished.

To her annoyance, there was only the answer phone to talk to when she dialled Tim's number. No doubt he would still be at the office poring over a set of books. Either that, or on some errand for his domineering mother. Rebecca sighed and left a brief message before she hung up in disgust.

As she left the kitchen, Martin entered the hall from the living-room.

"That was quick," he commented with a raised eyebrow.

"What was?"

"Your chat with the intended."

Rebecca ignored his amused smile and went to the stairs. Clearly his resolve for better relations had weakened and his curiosity had spurred him to further probing.

"Becky."

The huskiness of his voice made her steps falter. He moved close to her, his arm on the banister preventing her escape, as his hand cupped her cheek.

She slapped his hand away, alarmed that her skin tingled from his touch.

"What game are you playing now?" she hissed in the dark hallway.

"Why isn't the intended here with you, breaking the good news?"

"He's working."

"At this time?"

"An accountant's life is a busy one," she remarked lightly and tried to push past him without success. "We don't have to be together every waking moment."

"Really?" Martin's body moved inexorably closer to hers. "And what about sleeping moments?"

Rebecca flushed with anger. "I beg your pardon?"

"Are you living with him, Becky?" he whispered in her ear, his breath warm as it fanned her skin. "You don't sleep with him, do you?"

"How dare you?" she seethed with anger at his taunt.

His hand brushed against her neck and his gaze held hers. "He can't be any sort of man if he hasn't tried to take you to bed."

"Then what does that make you?" Rebecca snapped with cold fury as she pushed his away with all her strength.

Martin's eyes glinted like hardened steel, but she was free, and she took the chance to run up the stairs and escape him. When she reached the sanctuary of her room, she locked the door and slumped against it, her hands covering her face. Why did she still react to him? Why couldn't he leave her alone?

After a fitful sleep, Rebecca rose just before dawn. Whatever Damian and Jo might think, she could not stay and face Martin again — at least not until she had put the shock of yesterday into perspective.

Cursing her cowardliness, Rebecca left a hurriedly scribbled note promising to ring, collected her belongings and quietly let herself out of the cottage.

The drive home stretched before her, and she put a tape into the deck for company and to help her try and blot out her confused, uneasy thoughts. When she arrived at her bungalow, she dumped her bag in her bedroom, went to the kitchen for coffee, and then curled up on the settee.

There had been many days over the darkest months when she had been amazed at her fortitude, the fierce fighting spirit she had not known she possessed. Why, when there had been greater trials she had faced and overcome, had she run from a confrontation with Martin? Perhaps because he was the ultimate cause of all the rest?

A two-week holiday from work stretched before her, and she no longer looked forward to the time off. She could not even summon up the concentration for her study. It made her angry that no matter how hard she tried, Martin's image and the taunt of his words remained at the forefront of her mind.

The rest of the day was spent in ruthless spring cleaning — anything to give her something to do and take her mind off her worries. Tim rang her from work, and she felt guilty she was in such a bad mood. She could hear the disapproval in the business-like tone of his voice and endeavoured to be more cheerful. She even promised to go with him to his mother's to break the news of their engagement.

In the evening, she realised she could not put off the promised call to her brother, but was relieved when she heard Jo's cheerful voice on the end of the line.

"Rebecca! You must have left at the crack of dawn!"

"Yes, I am sorry, but . . . Well, I wanted to get home," she finished lamely.

"I'm not surprised. You have just become engaged, after all!" Jo teased. "You must bring Tim down for the week-end soon."

"I'll see what we can do."

Rebecca was annoyed with herself for taking the easy way out and allowing Jo to believe Tim was the reason for her sudden departure.

"It was wonderful to see you," Jo continued. "If Damian's patients ever give him any time off, we'll come up for a visit."

"Is Damian there?"

"No, he's at the surgery. Oh, blast, there's the doorbell. I'm sorry, Rebecca, I'll have to dash. We'll be in touch soon."

After she hung up, Rebecca had a long soak in the bath and decided on an early night. Her concentration had evaporated and there would be no point in study while she was in this frame of mind, she knew.

When she woke in the morning, she did not feel rested. A dull ache throbbed in her head, a warning to her, Rebecca acknowledged as she washed and dressed. Her night had been filled with dreams of Martin. In the cold light of day, she realised she had been fooling herself that she had put Martin and the past from her mind.

A traitorous part of the old Rebecca, pushed away behind doors she had hoped would remain closed for ever, still desired him. It was an admission that devastated her. It made a lie of all she had achieved, a mockery of the life she had built for herself.

Her head tight with stress and tension, Rebecca let herself out of the bungalow and drove to see her best friend, Caroline, who ran her parents' riding stables a few miles away.

When she pulled into the yard, Caroline ran to meet her.

"Rebecca, I've been dying to see you," she exclaimed, her neatly cut, dark brown bob swinging about her face and her hazel eyes shining with excitement. "It seems ages since you were here!"

"Exactly four days," Rebecca corrected, amused at her friend's gift of exaggeration.

Caroline linked her arm with hers and marched her into the yard. "You must see my new horse. He is absolutely wonderful! I can't wait to begin working with him. Of course, he's only five, but he's over sixteen hands, well muscled, and he looks huge! He's going to make a fabulous eventer."

Rebecca listened as Caroline chattered enthusiastically, but her fingers went unconsciously to the ache at her temple. When they arrived at the box, she peered dutifully inside. The dark, iron-grey gelding looked at them and came to the door. His soft muzzle explored Rebecca's outstretched hand, and she swore she saw a look of resigned martyrdom in his chocolate-brown eyes as Caroline threw her arms around his neck,

"He is gorgeous," Rebecca praised as she rubbed his ears. It was easy to see how Caroline had become so devoted to her new friend in such a short time. "What's his name?"

"Would you believe, Charcoal Smudges?" Caroline pulled a face and giggled. "Anyway, he's become known to us as Smudge, and he doesn't seem to mind!"

They left the horse to his hay and Rebecca followed Caroline up to the house.

"Are you busy with your parents away for a whole month?"

"So-so." Caroline kicked off her boots and poured two cups of coffee before she sat at the kitchen table. "The schools haven't broken up yet — all hell will break loose when they do. The week-ends are hectic though, and I have a lesson in half an hour. Well then, what's your news?"

Rebecca fidgeted anxiously. "Tim and I are engaged."

"Oh."

"Is that all you can say?" Rebecca laughed as she watched the doubtful expression on her friend's face.

"It's all I can say that won't make you cross. You know what I think of him."

"You just don't like him because he's not a horsey person."

Caroline shook her head vehemently. "That's not true! He's not right for you, Rebecca, and in your heart you know it. He's just safe, isn't he?"

"No! I — "

"We've been friends since kindergarten, and you may try to fool yourself, but you don't fool me. I hope you'll think about this properly, because you are not being fair to Tim or yourself."

"I know what I'm doing," she replied with a stubborn set to her jaw.

Caroline did know her better than anyone, but she was prejudiced about Tim, had never liked him. Rebecca massaged her forehead then slid her hand into the hair at the nape of her neck.

"That's the second time you've done that since you arrived," Caroline commented with concern. "Are you all right?"

"Mmm, just a headache coming on."

"Rebecca, you shouldn't have come if you're not feeling well. I didn't know you were still having those headaches."

She shrugged and smiled. "Not so many now. It's nothing to worry about."

"When is your next check-up?"

"Next week," Rebecca answered with a sigh. The headaches and a slight limp when fatigued were the only lasting evidence of her accident. The headaches were debilitating, and she would discuss it again with her consultant. "I'll be fine, Caro."

Her friend's brow creased in a frown. "If you're sure. Did you enjoy your visit with Damian and Jo?"

"I didn't stay long," Rebecca told her and rose from the table to wash her cup at the sink. "They had . . . company."

"Anyone I know?" Caroline picked up her uneasy hesitation and sat forward, her chin cupped in her hand.

"Martin."

"Ahh!" Caroline's eyes widened with speculation. "So, that's it."

Cross with herself for imparting

the information, and annoyed with Caroline's immediate interest, Rebecca spun round. "That's what?"

"Why you are so on edge and have that haunted look in your eyes."

"Don't be ridiculous."

"He got to you, did he?"

"He didn't do anything of the sort," Rebecca denied hotly. "I have no interest in him whatsoever."

"So you say." An amused smile curved Caroline's mouth. "I just bet you ran like a frightened rabbit because you couldn't handle seeing him. You did, didn't you?" she challenged, but Rebecca made no reply. "You should give the guy a chance, you know."

"Why should I? You always take his part in everything, make out I am the only one at fault."

"I just think you should listen to his side of the story. From what you said, it was quite chivalrous of him not to take advantage of the situation," Caroline reasoned.

"You would think that, but you were

not the one who was humiliated and abandoned."

"Rebecca — "

She raised a hand to silence her friend. "Let's just forget it. It doesn't matter any more."

"Really?" Caroline smiled a secretive smile. "So why are you so touchy and defensive?"

"I'm not!"

"Fibber. You should sort this out, Rebecca, because you have a mental block on it. The sooner you come to terms with what happened and talk to Martin about it, the better it will be for you. Your quiet life with Tim is your means of escape, and — "

"That's enough, Caroline. I will not discuss it any further. I'm sorry if you can't accept my decision, but Martin was a figure in my past. Tim is my future," she asserted, trying to control her temper. "Now, if you'll excuse me, I need some fresh air — and you have your lesson, remember?"

The ache in her head had intensified

as she left the house and walked back towards the stables. She hated to argue with Caroline, but her friend's well-meant interference served to make things more complicated. That Caroline could be right, at least in part, she refused to admit. The prospect was too difficult to deal with.

"Rebecca!" Caroline called after her and ran to catch up. "I'm sorry, I didn't mean to upset you. I just want you to be happy and I think you are making a mistake."

"Caro — "

"I know, you don't want to hear it. All right, I won't say any more, but you can always talk if you want to."

Rebecca smiled. "Thanks."

"Would you like to take Smudge out for a ride?"

"You are kidding!" Rebecca stared in amazement. She knew what an honour it was for Caroline to let anyone ride one of her own horses, especially one she was as fond of as her latest acquisition.

68

"Take him," Caroline insisted. "The exercise will do him good."

When Caroline went off to greet her pupil, Rebecca saddled Smudge and left the stables by the bridle path to the hills. The countryside was looking beautiful with a riot of spring flowers, the air full of birdsong and fresh scents.

Rebecca enjoyed riding Smudge and had to agree that the horse was magnificent. He was impeccably behaved, full of power but kind and responsive to every light command. As they reached the rising ground, she gave him his head, and he stretched out with deceptive ease. When she slowed him and turned for the woods, she reached forward to pat the grey neck in front of her.

The crash hat she wore had begun to feel tighter on her aching head, and she turned for home, anxious to arrive back at the stables before the headache intensified. The pressure built up in gradual layers, and she felt pain behind her left eye.

When she rode into the yard, she realised she had been out longer than she had intended, as Caroline was just taking a new group of pupils into the indoor school. She waved before she dismounted, unsaddled Smudge and led him into his box. She brushed Smudge down and made sure he had water and a small feed. Then Rebecca took the tack to the tack room. It was blissfully peaceful and dark inside — a welcome relief as the sunlight hurt her eyes.

She sat down on a wooden bench that ran the length of one wall, and for several minutes, she practised the relaxation techniques she had been taught in an attempt to ease the tension in her neck and help with the pain. Her eye felt as if it were on fire, her head encased in a steel band.

A depressed scar ran several inches back from her brow and her fingers traced it, trying to soothe the discomfort. The blood pulsed in her brain and nausea gripped her stomach. She did not dare to try and stand. She pressed the palm of her hand over her eye, drew up her legs and rested her forehead on her knees, waiting for Caroline to come.

How much time passed, she didn't know. She heard a car draw up outside the gate, followed some moments later by the clatter of horses hooves as the lesson returned from the indoor school. Caroline's voice raised in surprised welcome reached her ears, and she sighed in grateful relief. It would not be long now.

Then another voice, hated and familiar, responded to Caroline's greeting.

"Hello, Caro, how are you?" Martin asked. "I've come to see you about buying horses."

"You've really done it then — gone back to the farm?"

"I really have!"

Rebecca heard Caroline laugh and the easy camaraderie between her friend and Martin played on her nerves. She wished she could attract Caroline's attention, but did not want to alert Martin to her presence.

"Is that Becky's car?" she heard Martin ask and her hopes were dashed. "Where is she?"

"Now you come to mention it, I've not seen her since she came back from her ride," Caroline informed, her voice edged with concern. "I hope she's all right. She wasn't feeling well earlier on."

"What's the matter with her?"

"Oh, eh, just a headache, I think. I'll find out where she is."

As their footsteps retreated, Rebecca concentrated on her breathing as the pain increased and she fought against it. After several more minutes, she heard Caroline's voice call her name and then the sound of their approach towards the tack room door.

4

CAROLINE stepped inside the tack room and switched on the electric light. From her position in the corner, Rebecca groaned at the unexpected brightness and the light immediately switched off.

"I'm sorry," Caroline apologised as she hurried across. "I didn't think."

She felt Martin approach, but she did not look up. She thought she would die a thousand deaths to have him witness this weakness.

"Becky?" His voice was soft, his warm hand gentle on her cheek.

"Go away," she mumbled as she pushed his hand aside. She heard them move away and start whispering. "And don't talk about me as if I'm not here."

"I'm taking you home," Martin announced in an authoritative voice.

"Can you stand?"

"Leave me alone."

"Be quiet, for once, and do as you're told."

"Please, Rebecca," Caroline interjected. "I feel awful because I didn't make you go home this morning."

"It's not your fault, Caro," she reassured in a husky whisper.

When she tried to rise to her feet, she swayed unsteadily, and Martin's strong hands were immediately there to support her.

"Caroline, take my keys and open the doors," he instructed, then he swung Rebecca into his arms.

Rebecca held herself stiffly and was about to protest when they left the tack room and the full glare of the sun assaulted her. She moaned involuntarily as pain stabbed at her, and turned her face to Martin's shoulder. He felt safe and comforting, and the masculine scent of him was both familiar and disturbing.

Their departure was a blur on her

consciousness. Martin set her in his Range Rover and did up the seat-belt, and she vaguely remembered Caroline's anxious goodbyes. The journey did nothing to help her nausea. She wanted to curl up in a dark hole and escape the pain . . . escape Martin.

"We're nearly there," he informed her softly after a short while.

Rebecca opened her eyes to slits and through the mists that cloaked her, realised where they were. "Martin, I don't live in the old house any more."

"What? I — Never mind now. Tell me your address."

Rebecca told him the location of her bungalow and fell silent. Martin brooded beside her, and she hated to think of the questions that would be forming in his mind. But she felt too wretched to worry about it now.

Soon, he pulled up outside the bungalow and came round to help her out. Meekly, she handed him her door key and he carried her inside.

"Where's your bedroom?"

His commanding tone brooked no argument, and she waved a hand down the corridor to the left and indicated a door at the end. He walked into the room and set her gently on the bed.

"Thank you, I'll be all right now," she told him and tried to inject some authority into her voice.

Martin ignored her and went across to the window to draw the curtains and block out the light. "Get undressed and into bed."

"I — "

"Do it," he interrupted. "Or I'll do it for you."

He laughed wryly as she kicked off her boots, and then left the room. When she stood up, she wobbled, so she quickly sat down again and took off her clothes. She pulled a baggy T-shirt from under her pillow and slid it over her head, then crawled gratefully between the cool, cotton sheets that were a balm to her heated skin.

"I've brought you some water,"

Martin said as he returned to the room. "Do you have something you can take?"

"In the bathroom. The bottle with the red spot on the lid."

He was back almost before she realised he had gone. He sat on the edge of the bed. "Are these the ones?" he queried and she looked at the bottle and nodded. "How many?"

"Two."

Martin tipped them out and helped her to sit up, his hand firm between her shoulders as he supported her. She took the pills and the glass of water then sank back against the pillows.

"Is there anything else I can get you?"

"No, thank you. You don't have to wait any more."

"Just try to relax and get some sleep."

He made no move to get up, and although Rebecca wanted to protest, she could not find the strength. Martin eased her hand from her brow and his fingers replaced it, soft, cool and comforting as they worked over her skin, across her brow and temple into her hair in gentle movements. Their effect soothed her. She began to relax and regulate her breathing patterns, strangely reassured by his presence and concern.

She dozed fitfully, aware deep in her subconscious of acute disappointment when Martin's touch was withdrawn. The oblivion of sleep was denied her. Her head felt as if it would split right open and she wished she could escape the pain, that the medication would work more speedily.

Disorientated, her eyes flicked open, became accustomed to the darkness, and picked out Martin's figure as he sat on a chair near the bed. When he realised she was awake, he moved towards her and the bed depressed under his weight. His hand brushed some strands of fringe back from her forehead and she closed her eyes at the feel of his fingers against her skin.

"You're still here," she murmured, and blinked against the sudden tears that pricked her eyes.

Why had he stayed? Why should he care about her now? She turned her face away from his all-seeing gaze to hide the tracks of moisture as the tears won their freedom and slid between her lashes. She drew in a ragged breath, angry at her loss of self-control.

Why did she have to weaken now? Where was the spirit that had seen her through the fight of the last three years? It had deserted her in the face of Martin's unexpected consideration — and she feared what she may reveal to him. She hated this weakness and hated that he, of all people, should be a witness to it.

"Do you want me to get in touch with anyone?"

Rebecca shook her head.

"What about a doctor?" he queried softly.

"No."

"Not even Damian?"

"No," she said again. "I'll be all right in the morning."

Martin expelled a long, shaky breath and his fingers continued to brush back her hair. "Can't you take anything else?"

"They'll work eventually." She attempted to steady her voice that sounded husky to her own ears. "Is there any water?"

"Of course." Martin reached out to the bedside cabinet and handed her the glass, supporting her as she took a few sips. "All right?"

"Thank you."

His eyes glinted in the darkness of the room, and she bit her lip to try and stem the tears that gushed more insistently from her eyes. She despised her slump into self-pity and fought to regain her courage. Her voice trembled as she looked away from him once more.

"I'm sorry."

The back of his fingers trailed down her cheek and encountered the wetness.

"Oh, Becky," he murmured, his voice gruff with sympathy and concern.

Gentle hands turned her and pulled her towards him. She tried to resist, but she hadn't the will, and allowed herself to be held against the strong warmth of her body. She buried her face in his chest, fresh tears wetting the fabric of his shirt.

"It's all right," Martin comforted. He continued to talk to her, soft, meaningless words that helped her relax as his hand smoothed over her hair.

Of their own volition, her hands slipped around his neck and she wallowed in his strength. For now, it did not matter it was Martin. She would worry about it later.

"I'm sorry," she mumbled again.

"Stop apologising."

When he pulled back from her, his lips brushed in a soft caress against her cheek and left her skin tingling. His hands eased her away from him and she lay back against the pillows.

"Turn over," he told her.

"What?"

"Turn over."

Bemused, she rolled on to her side with her back to him, startled when he lay down behind her. One arm came to rest across her waist, the other on the pillow, his fingers returning to their soothing rhythm on her brow.

Rebecca licked her lips and opened her mouth to protest. "Martin — "

"Sssh," he murmured against her ear. "Try and sleep, sweetheart . . . "

★ ★ ★

When she woke in the morning, she lay for a moment, her brain slow to replay the events of the previous day. She felt drained and exhausted after the attack, despite eventually enjoying an uninterrupted night's sleep. She did not want to deal with thoughts of Martin.

She groaned as her sluggish mind reviewed the way she had turned to him for comfort. If only she could pretend it had all been a dream, she thought, as she pulled the covers over her head. At least he was no longer here to witness this further humiliation.

With reluctance, she glanced at her clock beside the bed and was surprised to find it was almost nine. She had not slept so late for months. Rebecca groaned again as she remembered she was supposed to be going with Tim to see his mother. It was the last thing she would wish for this morning. She needed to be in full fettle for an audience with Mrs Stevens.

So far, she had managed to get along passably well with Tim's mother, but how the woman would view the intended marriage, Rebecca was not sure. As far as Mrs Stevens was concerned, Tim was her boy, tied to the proverbial apron strings, and Rebecca doubted that another female in prominent rôle in his life would be welcomed. It was time that Tim asserted himself, and she would give him her support and encouragement.

Rebecca got up and went to the

bathroom to wash and clean her teeth. Her mouth felt dry, with an aftertaste from the medication. To her own eyes, her face appeared pale in the bathroom mirror and there were dark circles beneath her eyes. She fluffed her tousled hair into place with her fingers as she walked to the kitchen.

The smell of freshly-made coffee escaped as she pushed open the swing door, and a frown of puzzlement creased her brow. She stepped into the room then halted so suddenly that the door swung shut and bumped her in the back. She jumped in surprise and frowned again at the smile of amusement on Martin's face.

"You — " She cleared her throat and began again. "I thought you had gone."

He looked relaxed as he sat at the breakfast bar reading the newspaper

"I was not about to leave you," he replied as he refolded the paper and set his gaze on her in total concentration.

"That would make a change. It never

bothered you before," she muttered darkly as she moved to pour herself some coffee.

"I'm quite capable of helping myself to coffee," she protested, a snap in her voice.

"Do as you are told," Martin commanded. "You look dreadful."

"Thank you so much."

Rebecca sat down with reluctance and absently stirred some sugar into the cup that he passed to her. His continued presence in her home was unexpected. She was concerned that Martin, always watchful and speculative, would question her until he had drawn answers to the questions that had no doubt formed in his mind. Answers she had no wish to give.

"You're going to wear a hole in that cup," Martin teased.

Rebecca returned the spoon to the saucer with measured care. "There's no need for you to stay any longer."

"Such gratitude."

"I am grateful," she responded,

annoyed at the hint of mockery in his voice. "You were kind, but as you can see, I am quite all right now."

Martin's narrowed gaze studied her pale face. "That is a matter of opinion," he riposted before his tone became more gentle. "How are you feeling?"

"Fine, thank you." Her answer was shorter than she intended but he didn't seem to notice.

"What would you like for breakfast?"

"Oh, I don't have time for anything but coffee. I have to get ready."

He frowned and slid a detaining hand behind the knot of her dressing-gown.

"Ready for what?"

"I'm going out for the day, with Tim," she enlightened him as she struggled in vain to free herself from his hold.

"You most certainly are not."

His proprietorial air sparked her temper. "How dare you tell me what to do! This is my house, my life, and

86

I'll do as I damn well please."

"Be sensible, Becky. A fool can see that you are not up to it — no doubt Tim will as well."

"And what is that supposed to mean?" she bristled and tried to ease the defensiveness from her voice. "I am quite able to make my own arrangements."

"I'll talk to Tim, tell him you're not well."

"No!" Rebecca protested too quickly and groaned at the interest that darkened his eyes to grey. "I mean, I'm sure you have your own business to attend to, so why don't you just leave now? You've over-played your Good Samaritan part."

Martin's eyes flashed a warning of his submerged anger and she swallowed anxiously. She had no wish to provoke him. If only he would just go.

"Maybe I am losing patience," he told her in a hardened voice. "Maybe if you are feeling better, we should have a little talk."

"I don't think we have anything to talk about."

"Don't you? Well, believe me, you have some explaining to do."

"Such as?" Rebecca lifted her chin with more bravado than she felt and tried once more to extricate herself from his hold, but his hand merely tightened its grip, anchoring her in place.

"Such as why you are living here and not in the old house, why you are having these terrible headaches, why your bathroom cabinet has more pills in it than a pharmacy."

"You have no right to harass me and question me like this. You are not my keeper."

"Then maybe it is about time you had one."

They stared at each other in silence for several moments. His eyes looked into hers and she wished she had the mental strength to break the mesmering hold on her. Her heart hammered in her chest and her anxiety brought a light flush of colour to her paper-white cheeks. With alarm, she realised he was moving inexorably closer. She tried to back away from him, but the breakfast bar prevented her retreat.

It was the sudden, insistent ring of the doorbell that finally made him release his hold on her, and Rebecca had never imagined she would feel so grateful to hear that sound.

"That will be Tim," she told him, unable to hide her relief.

"I'll get it. You sit down and finish your coffee."

"No!"

She tried to catch hold of his arm, but he was gone. She slumped down on the stool and dreaded the scene about to take place on her front door step. Tim would pull himself up to his total height of five feet ten, which was inches shorter than Martin's more imposing frame. His dark-blond hair would be meticulously trimmed, his clothes neat and correct. Tim did not like anything to be out of place or contrary to his expectations, so he would be flustered when Martin, wild and rakish in comparison, opened the door to him.

His brown eyes would flick nervously as he felt at a disadvantage, and he would push his glasses higher up the bridge of his nose and speak in the clipped tones he used when dealing with something displeasing or untoward.

As the picture came to her mind, Rebecca immediately felt guilty at her disloyalty. Tim may not have Martin's blatant masculinity, but looks were not everything, and in personality and temperament, Tim was everything Martin was not. She heard their voices as they moved into the bungalow.

"I'm afraid she's not dressed yet," Martin drawled in deliberate provocation that had Rebecca slipping from the bar stool and running to meet them.

"Who exactly are you?" Tim demanded in an aggrieved voice. "What are you doing here?"

"I stayed the night. I'm a friend of the family."

Rebecca seethed with fury as Martin continued in his rôle of tormentor. She pushed open the door of the sitting-room but both men had their backs to her.

"I am Rebecca's fiancé — "

Martin chuckled. "So I understand."

"Will you tell her I'm here?" Tim's voice had risen and he was clearly at a loss. Rebecca did not blame him.

"I'm here," she hissed as she stepped into the room, angry spots of colour on her face. She glared at Martin, her fury increasing as he winked at her, unrepentant.

"Rebecca, why aren't you ready?" Tim asked as he kissed her chastely on the cheek. "You know Mother hates to be kept waiting."

"I'm sorry, I overslept. I had a headache yesterday and — "

"Another one?" Tim queried impatiently with an annoying lack of concern and Rebecca groaned as she saw Martin's gaze narrow.

"I think it would be best if she rested today," Martin intervened with determination. "Don't you?"

"Martin, I'm quite all right."

Tim looked at her with a frown. "You do look very pale, darling, and I know how lousy you feel after an attack. When I explain, I am sure Mother will understand," he added doubtfully and pushed his glasses up his nose. He glanced at his watch. "I'd better go. Best not to be late under the circumstances!"

Rebecca smiled and walked with him to the door. "I am sorry about today."

"Don't be silly. I just hope you'll soon feel better." He kissed her gently on the lips and then pulled back with a frown. "Who is that man, Rebecca?"

"He's Damian's friend, up from Devon to see Caroline about some horses," she improvised.

"I don't feel happy about him staying here, Rebecca."

92

"He is not staying here," she snapped impatiently, cross at his properness. "He brought me back from Caroline's yesterday when I wasn't well, that's all."

"But he stayed the night?"

"Yes, I suppose he did. I expect he thought Damian would want him to keep an eye on me." She sighed and lowered her lashes. "Hadn't you better go?"

"Yes, yes I must. Take care of yourself. I'll ring you later on."

Rebecca closed the door gratefully and leaned against it, her eyes closed. When she opened them, it was to find Martin standing in the hall, his gaze on her, his expression intent.

"How dare you?" she berated him, giving vent to her suppressed anger. "You have no right to come here and start messing about with my life. You upset Tim with your stupid games."

"Ah, yes, the intended." He smiled with a mocking twist to his lips as he walked slowly towards her. "He was hardly what I expected. Why him, Rebecca?"

"Because — because he's good to me, I like him, I — "

"Like? Don't you love him?"

"Of course!" she corrected, flustered. "Why would I be marrying him otherwise?"

He trailed a finger down her cheek, making her skin burn. "I don't know yet, sweetheart. But I intend to find out."

5

MARTIN'S threat rang in Rebecca's ears long after he had gone. She was on tenterhooks, but as one day slipped into another and brought neither sight nor sound of him, she began to relax.

But she doubted that his words were idle ones. For some reason, known only to himself, Martin had returned to her life and decided to poke his nose into her business. She was determined to put a stop to it. There was no room in her life for Martin . . . and she would not allow him to disturb all she had achieved.

She had been to an event with Caroline over the week-end, and had been relieved when her friend had uncharacteristically failed to pass comment or even mention Martin's name. Tonight, she was coming to dinner, along with Tim, and Rebecca hoped that her friend's discretion would be maintained.

Rebecca checked her watch. She had plenty of time to shower and change before putting the finishing touches to the meal.

Tim arrived at the stroke of seven, as precise in his timekeeping as in everything else. He kissed her briefly, a pleasant, friendly kiss, but one which set no spark of passion inside her. She brushed the thought aside and went into the sitting-room to pour him a drink.

"How is your mother?" she queried as she handed him a glass of sherry.

"Oh, you know! Still upset not to have seen you last week. You know how she gets when plans are changed," Tim added with a laugh, but his discomfort was obvious. "She goes on a bit."

Rebecca could imagine. The woman was a tyrant, made worse because, for some reason Rebecca could not understand, Tim would not stand up for himself. In every other aspect of his life, he was efficient and successful.

"You should assert yourself," she suggested and watched him over the rim of her wine glass.

"I know." He smiled wryly. "But she isn't that well, and I don't like to upset her."

So that was it. Lonely and alone, she was holding on to Tim with an iron hand and probably a fair amount of emotional blackmail thrown in. She would have to think of a gentle plan of campaign . . . she was not about to marry his mother as well as him!

The doorbell rang and she went to answer it. Caroline stepped inside, appearing ill at ease, and Rebecca wondered what was wrong. As she was about to close the door and question her friend, Martin stepped out of the shadows and into the hall. She wanted to slap the self-satisfied smile from his face, but she held her temper by a thread, determined not to give him the satisfaction.

"Please go through," she invited coolly.

"Why, thank you, Becky, how very gracious," he murmured lazily, and gave a tiny bow before he handed her a bottle of wine. "Here, I brought this along to liven things up. Does Tim drink?"

Rebecca seethed at his taunts and grabbed Caroline's arm to drag her into the kitchen. "How could you?" she hissed.

"I'm sorry. He turned up to buy some horses and asked if he could stay for a couple of days. I could hardly leave him at home on his own."

"I'm sure he doesn't need a nursemaid," Rebecca snapped crossly. "You could have warned me."

"There wasn't time. Oh, heck, I am sorry, I just thought . . . Would you like us to leave?"

"Yes, I don't want him in my house, but it's too late now."

When they went through to join the men in the sitting-room, Tim was looking uncomfortable. Through angry eyes, Rebecca noticed that in contrast, Martin was relaxed and clearly enjoying himself. She dreaded to think what he had been saying to Tim. For the rest of the evening, she would be careful not to leave them alone. She did not trust Martin an inch.

Rebecca sat next to Tim on the settee and smiled encouragingly, but the wind appeared to have been knocked from his sails. Her gaze moved to Caroline. Her friend looked miserable, and Rebecca regretted her harsh words. Caroline meant well, and probably felt in a quandary, torn between her loyalty to her best friend and the easy camaraderie she had always shared with Martin. No doubt, she had some rose-tinted image in her mind and was disappointed the rift between Rebecca and Martin had not been repaired.

Inevitably, Rebecca's gaze was drawn to Martin. He watched her through slumbrous eyes, but the laziness was deceptive, she was certain. Behind that façade lurked a speculative, extra-sharp mind. As if he knew what she was thinking, his lips curved in amusement and a glint brightened his eyes to indigo blue.

"Perhaps we should have dinner now," she suggested with all the calmness she could muster. "Tim, would you carry the salad for me?"

"Of course, darling."

In the kitchen, she handed him a tray. He took it from her, then hesitated.

"What is he doing here?"

"Caroline brought him along, I'm afraid. I had no idea he was coming."

"I hate the way he looks at you."

"Don't be ridiculous!"

Tim bristled. "I'm not."

"Look, he's just playing games. Ignore him."

She went through to the dining-room and set another place at the table. Much to her surprise, the meal did not start out the disaster she envisaged. Caroline, no doubt upset at her faux pas, made a strenuous effort to lighten the atmosphere, and Rebecca was grateful. Martin appeared content to let matters slip along, but she was wary of his intentions, and feared that some devilment simmered below the surface, like a semi-dormant volcano preparing for a surprise eruption.

"So, Martin, how long are you planning on staying in this part of the world?" Tim queried, failing to inject the right amount of nonchalance into his voice.

"However long it takes for me to get what I want."

Rebecca looked up anxiously, afraid Tim had awakened the sleeping tiger. Her gaze snapped to Martin to find him watching her. She swallowed and hastily returned her gaze to her plate.

"You're a farmer, I believe?" Tim continued, and whilst his tone was not entirely derisive, it clearly displayed his incomprehension of animals, the way of life, work on the land.

Martin's eyes narrowed as he picked

up the thread of scorn in Tim's voice. "Of a sort."

"Eh, yes," Caroline interjected. "I'm helping Martin buy some horses for the stud he is starting."

"I'm glad," Rebecca allowed, unable to hide her interest or halt the memory of how he had confided his dream to her. Her curiosity was piqued despite her annoyance with him. "Thoroughbreds?"

"Some," Martin nodded. "But I'm not interested in breeding for racing. I want decent eventers, show jumpers and good riding horses, and hope to cross with Irish Draught, Trakaener and such like."

"Have you converted the whole farm to the stud?"

"No, it's still a mixed farm — at least for the time being." He smiled. "We'll see how things go."

"Have you given up your job then?"

Martin's eyes clouded to grey and she noticed a pained expression in them before he masked it. "You know

I've been planning this for a long time. Now seemed the right time to do it."

Rebecca felt sure he was hiding something, that it was not as simple as he made it sound. She was about to say something, but his expression daunted her. What had put such bitterness and hurt in those devastating eyes?

"You'll have to come down one day and look around," Martin suggested after a moment's silence and held her gaze.

She swallowed against a sudden constriction in her throat. She wanted to go and knew she could not. Disturbed by his gaze, she dragged her own away.

"Perhaps Tim and I will come down after we are married."

"Yes, if you would really like to, Rebecca," Tim agreed doubtfully.

"When is the happy day?" Martin drawled, his mood altered once more.

"Soon, I hope," Tim responded with welcome enthusiasm. "There are arrangements to be made, and naturally it will have to fit in with work."

Martin glanced at Rebecca, a mocking tilt to his lips. "Naturally!"

Annoyed, Rebecca remained silent. Tim's words had not been tactful, but she was not about to comment in front of Martin. He was causing enough tension on his own, and his tone caused Tim to frown, as if he was unsure whether or not Martin was making a fool of him.

"And what about Rebecca's work?" Martin asked now as he sat back in his chair and watched Tim attentively.

"Of course, as my wife, she won't need to work. Or slave away at her studies, will you, darling?"

Rebecca was stunned by his announcement. She had no intention of giving up her job, or her studies, so Tim would have to think again! His attitude amazed her, but she was unwilling to air the disagreement in public . . . especially with Martin amongst the audience.

Martin's eyes sharpened, alert and interested as he looked from her to Tim.

"What studies?"

Blast him! He would pick up on the one slice of information Tim had given away. The last thing she wanted was Martin meddling in her affairs.

"Psychology," Tim elaborated when Rebecca remained stubbornly silent.

The steel grey gaze turned its full attention on her. "I thought you said you had changed your mind about Psychology."

"I did," Rebecca confirmed, warmth in her face. "Now I've changed it again."

"Really?" Martin raised an eyebrow. "And why is that?"

"I — " She cast about desperately for a way to change the subject.

"As a friend of Damian's, you'll know, of course," Tim interrupted her hesitant beginning. "It wasn't possible to do the degree at the time, was it darling?" he went on, ignoring her frantic signals for him to keep silent. "Not after the —— "

"Have some more pavlova, Tim," Rebecca cut across him with haste, her voice too strident.

Tim had nearly blurted out things she had no wish for Martin to know . . . and he had piqued Martin's infernal curiosity into the bargain. The reflective grey gaze held her own for several uncomfortable moments. She had hoped time would lessen Martin's interest and dampen the speculation that had been evident the previous week. He had questions, he had said, and now, to her despair, he had reason for more.

Caroline came to her rescue, telling of her recent pursuit of a handsome, eligible competitor on the event circuit. She soon had them all laughing at her exploits, and Rebecca was heartily grateful for her intervention.

When they moved through to the sitting-room for coffee, she became tense once more. She tried to join in the conversation, but the touch of Martin's gaze seldom left her, and she grew more agitated as the minutes ticked by.

She looked at Tim, her friend, the man she had agreed to marry. She had grown used to him, she realised, as one did to an old pair of slippers, or a lifetime routine. Their relationship was predictable, unchallenging, unthreatening.

Her gaze flicked to Martin who sat relaxed in an armchair. Where Tim was comfortable, Martin was wild. Where Tim was dependable, Martin was mercurial. Where Tim was safe . . . Martin was exciting.

Rebecca swallowed in discomfort, ashamed at the direction of her thoughts. Perhaps she and Tim did not have an all-consuming passion, but they liked each other, began from the basis of friendship. She would make him happy, and one day, she would grow to love him. The admission shocked her, and she gave a sudden start, drawing the attention of the others. Martin's watchful gaze intensified. She coloured with embarrassment and smiled self-consciously.

"I was day-dreaming." She laughed uneasily.

When Caroline suggested it was time to leave, Rebecca barely restrained herself from leaping to her feet. She was eager to rush Martin from her home, and she was in no doubt that he knew, as his eyes sparkled with mocking amusement.

Tim shook hands in formal goodbye, as proper and courteous as ever.

"Perhaps we shall meet at the wedding."

"Perhaps!"

Disconcerted, Rebecca walked Caroline to the door. "I'll see you soon," she promised.

"Am I forgiven?"

"Not at the moment," she admitted, but a smile removed the sting from her words. "But you will be."

Caroline laughed and hugged her.

"Good luck tomorrow," she whispered in her ear.

"Thanks." Rebecca said. She had quite forgotten her appointment at the hospital the next day. She smiled as Caroline stepped outside, only to turn and discover Martin behind her. Instinct told her to move away, but her retreat was blocked, and his finger under her chin forced her to look up at him and into his eyes that appeared to glow with blue flames.

"Thanks for dinner, Becky. It's been an interesting evening! At least Tim appreciates your cooking if nothing else."

"Goodbye, Martin," she stressed, her voice harsh with anger.

"No, I don't think so," he murmured, a deep sensuousness in his voice that sent a prickle of awareness along her spine. He bent and pressed a firm kiss to her startled mouth, then drew away to look at her. A smile curved his lips — lips whose imprint she could still feel against her own. "Not goodbye, just goodnight."

Dumbfounded, she watched the car drive away, her fingers pressed to her mouth. Wearily, she closed the door and returned to the sitting-room with reluctance. There was still Tim to face.

"I'm glad that's over," he said when she walked into the room.

"You and me both."

She sat down in an armchair facing him, and felt that she looked at him for the first time. He was pleasant to look at. In fact, everything about him was pleasant, but as much as she cared for him, he did not excite her.

"Rebecca!"

"I'm sorry?" The impatience in Tim's tone made her look up. "Did you say something?"

"You haven't heard a word I've said, have you?"

She cursed her wayward thoughts and drew her attention back to Tim. "I was miles away. What did you say?"

"I said," Tim emphasised deliberately, "that I hope Martin will soon be on his way back to Devon."

"Yes."

"He seems a complicated chap. I can't make him out."

"Mmm," she murmured noncommittally. The last topic she wanted to talk about was Martin — especially now, especially with Tim.

"He fancies you."

"That's nonsense," she stated with conviction, the memory of his rejection emblazoned on her mind. "He has never been interested in me in the least."

"He watches you, Rebecca."

She lowered her gaze and studied the pattern on the carpet. "You are just imagining things."

"No I'm not. I don't want you seeing him again."

"I have no intention of seeing him," she replied, her voice terse as she attempted to maintain a hold on her frayed temper. "But even so, I do not appreciate being told what I can and cannot do."

Tim pushed his glasses up his nose and stared at her, twin spots of colour on his cheeks. "I am your fiancé, Rebecca."

"You do not own me, or control my free will. We can discuss, we can debate, we can compromise, but neither can dictate to the other what to do."

"You're tired." Tim stood up and buttoned his jacket. "We'll talk about it another time."

It infuriated her when he did that, and her voice was stiff with annoyance.

"Yes. And more besides."

"Such as?"

"Your ideas on my rôle as your wife."

"I thought I explained — "

"Very clearly," she interrupted. "In front of Caroline and Martin, you made it plain you thought I should be a good little girl and stay at home to be at your beck and call. Are you going to keep me tied to the kitchen sink, barefoot and pregnant?"

Tim flushed with embarrassed colour. "Don't be foolish."

"I have no intention of giving up my studying. It's important to me."

"I don't know what's got into you, Rebecca. You aren't yourself today." Tim walked to the door and turned to look at her, a frown of angry puzzlement in his eyes. "I have tickets for the theatre on Friday. I'll pick you up at seven and we can talk then."

"Thank you for asking," she muttered sarcastically. "Will I see you before then, or is work too pressing?"

"I'll call you." His tone rang with displeasure at her effrontery. He kissed her on the cheek, the atmosphere chilled between them as he left the house.

Was this the beginning of the end, Rebecca wondered when he had gone. She hated to row with him, did not want the disagreement to spoil their friendship. He just made her so mad.

Caroline's doubts and Tim's current attitude, did make her think . . . did she really know him at all? Had they as much in common as she once thought? Could she spend the rest of her life with him?

Concerned at the direction of her thoughts, she returned to the sitting-room to clear away the coffee tray. As she bent down to collect it, she noticed something beside an armchair in the corner. It was Martin's jacket! She picked it up and held it for a moment, feeling the leather beneath her fingers. It held a lingering trace of aftershave and Martin's masculinity. Angry with herself, she tossed it aside.

"Damn Martin, this is all his fault," she complained aloud to the empty house. "None of this would have happened if he hadn't come back."

6

"ALL right, all right, I'm coming," Rebecca yelled as the doorbell sounded for the third time.

She had just completed the exercise programme designed for her needs since her accident, and had spent the last twenty minutes on the exercise bicycle. Hot and tired, she had been about to enjoy an invigorating shower and early lunch before she went to the hospital for her check-up. Rebecca cursed this unforeseen intrusion and opened the front door with a sigh.

"'Morning, Becky," Martin's husky voice greeted her, his mouth curved in an amused smile as she stared at him in amazement.

"What are you doing here?"

"Can I come in?"

"No, you can't come in, I — " She

broke off as he pushed her gently into the hall, stepped inside and closed the door behind him. "What do you think you are doing?"

Martin observed her in silence, his eyes cobalt as his gaze travelled over her from head to toe and back again. She shifted under his intimate inspection, aware she was still dressed in her leggings and leotard, her hair swept back from her face with a blue ribbon.

"Nice outfit," he murmured.

As he moved closer, Rebecca backed cautiously down the hall. "Why have you come?"

"I forgot my jacket."

He even had the nerve to sound repentant at what had clearly been a deliberate omission. Rebecca fumed as she went to the sitting-room and snatched his jacket from the chair. She tossed it towards him. "Take it and go."

"Hardly a gracious welcome," Martin drawled, his eyes assessing her.

"Why should it be?"

"You knew I would come."

"Did I?" Her chin lifted in defiance as she met his gaze boldly. "And why is that? Because you so conveniently left your jacket behind? Hardly original."

"Because you are going to answer my questions," he corrected, a calm deliberation in his voice that made her nervous.

"I have nothing to say to you. Now, you will have to leave, because I have an important appointment and I have to shower and change."

Martin closed the gap between them and trailed a finger across her damp forehead before she could slap his hand away. He smiled. "Don't let me stop you. As the intended isn't here, perhaps I should scrub your back for you."

Rebecca sucked in an angry breath. "Not a chance," she snapped, unable to prevent the flush that reheated her face.

"Pity. Aren't you at least going to offer me some coffee?"

"Help yourself," she murmured ungraciously. She refused to bandy words with him any longer. "I don't have time to stand here and listen to your nonsense. See yourself out."

She marched to the bathroom and slammed the door, careful to lock it securely. Martin was not to be trusted. She stripped off her exercise gear and stepped under the cool spray. After she had washed her hair, she stepped out of the shower and dried herself vigorously before she returned to her room to dry her hair. She applied some moisturiser and lip gloss, then rubbed some oil into her weakened leg, her fingers trailing absently over the unsightly scar, before she dressed.

Rebecca checked her watch and decided she had time for an omelette before she went to the hospital. She was confident that even Martin, with his thick skin, would have taken the hint by now and gone.

She pushed open the kitchen door and breathed a sigh of relief when she found the room empty. Martin's mug had been washed and was upturned on the drainer. She smiled with relief, took down another mug and poured herself some coffee from the percolator on the worktop. A cry of alarm escaped her as two strong arms curled around her waist from behind. She felt the length of Martin's body against her back and stiffened in response.

"Mmm," he murmured huskily against her ear. "You smell nice."

"Take your hands off me."

Rebecca struggled to free herself from his hold. Her mug clattered to the sink and broke, spraying out in shards across the shiny steel. She thrust herself away from him, her face aflame. He let her go and watched her, his gaze intent on the play of emotions across her face.

"How dare you?" she fumed. "I thought I told you to go."

"And I told you we were going to talk."

"We are not going to talk, so you can take your questions with you and disappear. Now, I have to go out."

Martin stepped towards her, his eyes narrowed. "So I'll come with you."

"You will not!"

"Then I'll wait for you to come back."

Rebecca sighed and clenched her fists in despair. "Why can't you get it through your thick skull that I do not want to see you, do not want to talk to you?" she demanded, her irritation bringing a snap to her voice.

"Perhaps because I don't believe you."

"Then that is your problem, not mine."

"Becky," he said, his voice soft and cajoling as he reached out for her hand.

She knocked his arm aside and stepped away. "Don't Becky me. Just go away."

"And leave you with the intended? I don't think so." His eyes deepened to dark grey as he stared at her.

"Stop calling Tim that. It sounds ridiculous."

"The fact that you are even considering marriage to him is ridiculous."

"I don't think so."

"So, you are going to turn yourself into a good little housewife?"

She bridled at Martin's mocking tone and the half smile that played across his mouth. "What's wrong with that?"

"Nothing . . . if it's your choice." He moved to block her exit from the kitchen with his body. "I saw your expression last night when he spouted all that stuff about no wife of his working."

"There is such a thing as compromise," she retaliated but her lashes dipped to escape his gaze.

"But you've never discussed it, have you?"

Rebecca turned away from his challenge in confusion. She could not think straight when he was so close to her, when he showered her with arguments. He played skilfully on her insecurities and sowed unwelcome seeds of doubt.

"You don't love him," Martin told her with harsh bluntness.

"What makes you say that?"

"Because you never once asked for him when you weren't well, never asked for me to call him to be with you . . . but you murmured my name in the night when you tossed and turned and I held you in my arms."

"That was just because you were there. I didn't know what I was saying," she denied in a rush, warm colour flooding her cheeks.

His words brought back memories — painful memories of the first few days in hospital before Damian and Jo rushed back from their honeymoon in Canada. Days when, the nurses told her, she had called repeatedly for Martin — had called for him and he had not come.

While she was lost in thought, he moved to her and slipped an arm around her waist, anchoring her to him. She tried to resist, but he held her gently fast. He raised a hand and brushed the hair away from her face. Her skin tingled at the touch of his fingers, then he bent his head, his face close to hers, his breath fanning her cheeks. Rebecca swallowed and licked her lips nervously.

"So you feel nothing," he breathed, and the sensual thread of his voice sent a tingle down her spine.

"I'm engaged to another man, and I'm happy," she told him, her voice unsteady. "I want you to stay out of my life."

"You're lying to yourself, Becky. It isn't over between us."

"Nothing started, remember?" she taunted, unable to keep an edge of bitterness from her voice.

"Maybe I've changed my mind. Maybe I've decided to collect on what was offered."

A quiver of alarm shot through her. "Then you are three years too late."

"You think so?" The palm of his hand was firm on her cheek as he forced her to look at him. "I don't."

"What are you trying to prove?" she questioned. "That the girl you once rejected will not reject you? If that is the case, you are sorely mistaken, and if that dents your macho ego, it's just hard luck."

"Is that what you think this is about?"

"I do not begin to understand the workings of your mind but I will tell you something — " she began, and placed her hands on his chest to hold him away from her.

His gaze sharpened as he looked down at her. "And that is?"

"Three years ago, you told me I would thank you one day. I did not believe you then, but now I do. You were the biggest mistake of my life. I've learned from that mistake, and I am not about to repeat it."

"Then explain why you are so aware of me."

"Don't flatter yourself! If I appear ill at ease, it is because your presence reminds me what a fool I was to believe in a teenage infatuation. I am grateful to you for that much at least. My only regret is what I did to myself."

Martin's eyes narrowed to steel grey slits and his hold on her tightened.

"Tough words."

"Perhaps — but true ones." Her gaze faltered under the pressure of his.

"And Tim?" he mocked, his hand moving down to caress her throat, his thumb resting on the throb at the hollow. "Does his touch make your pulse race?"

"Don't!"

She raised a hand to his strong wrist to try and free herself, but he held her gently captive. Slowly, his mouth moved to brush hers, his lips tantalising in their light caress. Rebecca gasped at the sensation that sent a bolt of fire throughout her body. As his kiss deepened, her mind insisted she fight him, but the effect of his expertise weakened her resolve.

His fingers slid through her hair to hold her firm. She was aware of nothing but him. Involuntarily, her hands slid around his neck. But as Martin dragged his mouth from hers, his whispered words penetrated the fog in her brain.

"You still want me."

The hint of triumph in his voice acted like a bucket of icy water to her dazed senses. He had played with her again, toyed with her emotions to prove a point, and a wave of shame and anger swept over her. She had allowed him to do this to her again.

"No!" she cried, her voice ragged.

"Does he have this effect on you?" he breathed against her heated skin. "Does his kiss make your body tremble?"

With a superhuman effort, she pushed herself away from him. "Stop it!"

"Tell me."

"You are talking about lust and it means nothing."

"I'm talking about passion, and it means everything."

"No," she denied, a quiver running

through her as she tried to recover from the shock of his sensual onslaught. "Everything is when you have trust and kindness, friendship and loyalty. That's what Tim and I share."

Martin shook his head, his eyes intent and startlingly blue. "You're wrong, Becky. He won't make you happy. You don't love him. You may think all those things are enough, but without passion, you have nothing," he challenged taking her arm.

"Let me go," she insisted angrily, disturbed by his words.

She twisted her arm against his hold and struggled for release. Unable to stand the full force of his gaze, she dragged her own away and looked wildly round the kitchen. She noticed the clock on the wall, remembered where she was meant to be, at the hospital, not here suffering Martin's assault on her senses.

"I have to go."

"When you've answered my questions."

"Can't you understand? I have an

appointment I can't miss."

His eyes looked into hers as if he doubted her, then his expression softened. "If I let you go, will you agree to talk before I go back to Devon?"

"There is nothing to talk about — "

"Becky," he warned as the grip of his fingers tightened. "The choice is yours."

Her gaze flickered to the clock and anxiety bettered her judgment. "Oh, all right."

"When?"

"I don't know. Soon," she agreed with deep reluctance. She licked her lips, still sensitised from his kiss, her eyes wide with concern where he did not immediately release his hold. "You said you would let me go."

His grip relaxed after a long moment and his gaze bored into hers. "I don't break a promise. Make sure you don't break yours."

★ ★ ★

Caroline tapped a finger on the top of the cluttered desk in the riding school office. "Earth calling Rebecca. Anyone home?"

Rebecca started as her friend jerked her from her introspection and she stared across the desk, a wry smile on her face. "I'm sorry, I was miles away."

"I gathered!" Caroline laughed. "You were going to tell me how you got on at the hospital yesterday, remember?"

"Fine, making good progress, as they say. You know the kind of thing."

Caroline frowned, a sharpness in her hazel eyes as she rested her elbows on the desk. "You don't seem very pleased."

"Oh, I am, really. I was given a thorough going over — my leg can still feel it!" She grinned, rubbing her left shin. "The doctor said everything was going well."

"And the headaches?"

Rebecca shrugged and lowered her

gaze. "He said he was not unduly worried."

"What else did he say?" Caroline pressed as she picked up on Rebecca's hesitation.

Rebecca fiddled with a pencil on the desk. "Just that they could have been affected with any kind of stress or emotional upset."

"Ah! I think we both know what that means." Caroline sat back in her chair and bit her lip. "Rebecca, if you could only sort this out."

"There's nothing to sort out."

"Can't you see how much better it would be if you talked about it and let it all go?"

"I can't, Caro," Rebecca sighed, a crack in her voice. "It brings it all back, just seeing him. Oh," she exclaimed and waved a hand as Caroline began to interrupt, "not only the whole stupid business with Martin himself, but afterwards — the accident. I can't go through it all again."

"But you are going through it. You're

tormenting yourself. I've never known anyone with as much courage as you, Rebecca. How you coped and fought and conquered one difficulty after another. You've achieved so much. Why stop now and keep it bottled up?"

She was touched by her friend's concern, and knew that without Caroline, she would have found the rehabilitation much harder. But what she was suggesting . . .

"Look," Caroline continued, "you've tied up what happened with Martin with the accident and afterwards. Until you admit that and deal with it, it will come back to haunt you."

"I don't know."

"I know I promised not to say any more, but this business of marrying Tim is just an extension of the feelings you've locked away. Your relationship with him is unchallenging. You feel in control of yourself and that makes you feel safe. Your emotional well-being is not in someone else's hands. Oh,

Rebecca," she pleaded with a sigh. "Please think about this. I care too much about you to see you make such a huge mistake."

"I'll see, Caro. And I do appreciate your concern. It's just that . . . " Her voice trailed off.

"I know, you are just too stubborn to lay Martin's ghost to rest, and too afraid you still care about him and will get hurt again."

Rebecca stared at her friend in confusion, unwilling to acknowledge the truth of the words. "I thought I was the one who was supposed to be doing the psychology."

Caroline smiled. "You will think about it though?"

"Yes, all right."

As if she had any option, Rebecca thought to herself. Her mind was in turmoil, and she wanted time to be by herself to try and think things through with a calm head.

"Caro, is it OK if I go for a ride?"

"Of course. I've worked Smudge this

morning, but you can take your pick of the rest, except Fanny. I need her for a private pupil in fifteen minutes, otherwise I would come with you."

Rebecca stood up and walked to that door that led to the yard. She paused for a moment, uncertain, her voice soft with enquiry. "Martin?"

"He went over to Guildford to look at a mare early this morning," Caroline informed her.

Rebecca sighed with relief. She needed more time before she saw him again. "I'll probably ride over to the lake," she murmured, gazing beyond the stable blocks to the curve of the North Downs in the distance.

"Good place for a think."

"Something like that." Rebecca turned to smile at her friend, waved a farewell and set off for the tack room.

After she had saddled her favourite horse, a dark-brown thoroughbred gelding called Silhouette, she led him across to the concrete mounting block, her leg still stiff from her intensive hospital examination. She rode out of the yard and took the bridle-path to the woods where the last, late bluebells lingered.

She kept to a walk, Silhouette keen and yet obedient, and the burden of her problems weighed heavily on her mind. And not only Martin, she allowed, but also her growing unease about Tim. Was she doing the right thing? Or, as Caroline had suggested, had she merely convinced herself she was happy? Was marrying Tim an excuse? Was she running away?

Unsettled by her thoughts, she left the wood and took the long, circuitous route to the lake. She trotted Silhouette along a quiet country lane before she turned on to another bridleway, bordered by thick beech hedges, that ran down between two fields of oilseed rape. She hated to see the acres of artificial gaudy yellow splashed across the countryside.

As the path opened before her, she allowed the horse to break into his easy canter, enjoying the feel of the fresh breeze against her face. Finally, she brought him back to a walk, giving him a loose rein as she patted the warm, smooth arc of his neck, and turned at the junction of the path into another wood. Soon she was out of the trees and skirting the meadow that bordered the lake.

What was she going to do about Martin? He had forced a promise from her that she would answer his questions and there was no doubt he would hold her to it. But what could she tell him? And why was he interested after all this time?

She sighed with frustration and turned Silhouette on to the track that hugged the water's edge. The lake nestled at the foot of the hills and Rebecca halted to watch a heron, patient and motionless as it hunted for fish.

Her thoughts continued to plague her. If only Martin would leave her alone, stop confusing her, would go back to wherever he had disappeared to these last three years. She did not want the past raked up. She wanted to forget about the accident, forget her foolish infatuation with him.

Martin had told her with cruel bluntness there could never be anything between them — had made it all too clear she was not his type. She closed her eyes against the sudden thought of him with another woman, dismayed that it should bother her.

"Stop it," she rebuked herself. She must not think about him. He meant nothing to her — as she meant nothing to him. He was toying with her, satisfying an itch because she refused to pander to him, to fall at his feet again. Her fingers had been burned once before, surely she was not fool enough to test the heat of the flames a second time?

The sound of a horse's hooves interrupted her thoughts and she turned, shading her eyes from the sun with one hand. Her shoulders slumped as she recognised Martin. He approached from the other side of the meadow having taken the quickest route from the stables. As he slowed his bay mare and walked to join her, Rebecca returned her gaze to the heron, who, disturbed, rose ponderously from the rushes, tucked in his long neck, and flapped farther down the side of the lake.

"'Morning," Martin greeted as he halted by her side.

"How did you find me?"

"I wheedled the information from a reluctant Caroline."

"What do you want?" she asked, her voice flat, tired. "Why follow me here?"

"I'm going back to Devon this afternoon."

Rebecca slanted a glance at him. "So?"

"So, I think it's time we had that talk, don't you?"

"I — "

"You gave your word," he reminded her.

She dragged her gaze from his, disturbed by his strength of determination. Beneath her, Silhouette scraped the ground with a hoof and tossed his head impatiently, and she ran her hand down his neck. She drew a deep breath and faced him with resignation. The sooner she imparted the information, the sooner he would go away.

"What exactly do you want to know?"

"Suppose you start by telling me why your life has taken a dramatic about turn."

"I had an accident," she told him bluntly. "The morning after you walked out on me, I stepped under a bus."

7

BEFORE Martin could react, Rebecca urged Silhouette forward and cantered along the path and up a gentle slope towards a large oak tree that crowned the centre of a hilly mound. Her heart thudded against her ribs. Why had she blurted it out to him like that?

"Rebecca! Rebecca, wait, Damn it!" he shouted after her, his angry voice carrying across the distance she had placed between them.

She heard him behind her, closing the gap, and as he drew alongside, he leaned across and grabbed hold of her reins, forcing her to stop.

"Let go!"

He ignored her protest and dismounted in one fluid motion, his hand holding Silhouette's bridle. His face was thunderous. A flicker of fear ran through her at the biting intensity in his narrowed grey eyes.

"Get down."

"No."

She wrestled to be free and tugged at the reins, but he reached up and physically yanked her from the saddle. She let out an involuntary gasp as she reached the ground and her weak leg almost gave way beneath her. She stumbled, and Martin put out a hand to steady her.

"What is it? What's the matter?"

"Nothing," she snapped, annoyed at her weakness as she pulled away from him, unable to disguise her slight limp. She stepped back in alarm as he moved towards her and went to take her arm. "No! Don't touch me. Just leave me alone."

"The hell I will. You don't say something like that and just go off, damn it." He dragged his fingers through his hair in a gesture of agitation, his grey eyes stormy as he fought to control his temper.

"What happened?"

Rebecca leaned against the trunk of the tree and twisted the reins in her nervous fingers. "I fractured my skull, cracked a few ribs, and broke my left leg in four places," she told him, her voice emotionless.

Martin swore under his breath, his face pale and grim as he looked at her.

"I'm sorry, I didn't know, I — "

"You can't pretend you care now," she interrupted hotly, all her old anger and hurt bubbling to the surface. "You made the situation perfectly clear three years ago and you've made no effort to communicate until now."

"I've been away," he pointed out tersely, anger emanating from him. "I — "

"Spare me the details of your latest exotic vacation practising your charms on the local females. I've heard it all before and I'm not interested."

"Rebecca, listen, you don't understand."

"No, *you* don't understand. I have my own life now and you are not part of it. I have been through enough over you."

His eyes hooded, the irises slate grey. "Are you saying that you deliberately walked under that bus because I did not fall in with your scheming?"

"I — " Rebecca swallowed in shock and confusion. "It just happened, I wasn't thinking — "

A muscle pulsed along his jaw, and when he spoke, his voice was dangerously calm. "You blame me."

It was a statement, not a question, and Rebecca stared at him in surprised bewilderment. Before she had time to assemble her thoughts and respond to his clipped accusation, he spun away from her with a gesture of disgust and swung himself effortlessly back into the saddle.

"I'll leave you alone, Rebecca. Have your life, marry your excuse of a fiancé, vegetate — if you call that living. There's nothing more to be said between us."

Stunned, Rebecca watched him go,

too proud and fearful to call him back. He rode away from her without a backward glance. She watched until man and horse were a speck in the distance, silent tears sliding down her cheeks. Silhouette nuzzled her hair softly and she stroked his nose.

"I've got what I wanted," she told the horse as she buried her face against his neck. "I've driven him away."

So why did she now feel so wretched?

Tired and desolate, Rebecca rode slowly back to the stables. She felt numb, devoid of life, of spirit, her actions mechanical as she returned Silhouette to his box and saw to his needs. As she was carrying the tack across the yard, Caroline came to meet her, an angry frown on her face.

"What did you say to Martin?" she demanded.

Rebecca continued into the tack room, put the saddle away and hung up the bridle. "Why?"

"He looked ghastly when he arrived back here. He couldn't pack his things and leave quickly enough. What have you done?"

"Nothing." Rebecca bit her lip, unable to meet her friend's gaze as a stab of guilt lanced through her. "What did he say?"

"Nothing," Caroline quoted back at her, an uncharacteristic snap in her voice.

"Caro — "

"I asked him what happened, but he wouldn't tell me," she continued. "He was hardly in the mood to talk. He just said it was all over."

Rebecca blinked back a fresh welling of tears. "It is. It has been for a long time."

Caroline stood at the door shaking her head, her voice full of sadness and exasperation. "You're a fool, Rebecca. A complete and utter fool."

★ ★ ★

As the days passed, Rebecca became more morose. She had made such a

144

mess of everything. She could no longer bury her head ostrich-like in the sand, that much was clear. It was time to face up to things.

The hours of soul-searching drained her. Martin had proved that she was not sufficiently committed to Tim to marry him. How could she when she desired another man? All the things Caroline had said now made sense. She had just been too stubborn, too fearful to admit it. She had been running away, using her accident as an excuse to hold on to her anger and bitterness at Martin for rejecting her — protecting herself from further hurt. And now she had used that anger to hurt him and push him away.

She was mortified she had allowed him to believe she blamed him for what had happened to her. Perhaps a part of her had wanted to punish him for the humiliation and disillusionment he had caused her? Whatever the reason, her behaviour was unforgivable. How could she have done that to him?

But the most painful thing of all was that she still wanted him.

She had made excuses and seen little of Tim, and when she returned to work, the atmosphere between them was cool. He had been a good friend since she had joined the firm, she had no wish to hurt him, and it was not his fault she was so contrary. She tried to explain as much to him over a quiet lunch.

"I really am sorry, Tim. I value your friendship. I care about you, but I can't marry you."

Tim sat across the table from her, his mouth twisted with disapproval.

"It's him, isn't it? Martin?"

"Only in part." Rebecca sighed. She knew she was doing the right thing, for both of them; it was just so hard. "I can never be the sort of wife you want, Tim. You deserve so much more than I can give you. It wouldn't be fair. I would only make you miserable, and I don't want that."

With a mixture of sadness and relief,

she slipped his ring off her finger and handed it back She truly hoped he would be happy, would find someone who would love him — who would please his mother.

Despite the fact that they had reached an understanding, it proved awkward and uncomfortable seeing Tim each day at work. A restlessness and dissatisfaction grew inside her. With her financial affairs on the straight and narrow, she decided she would leave her job and concentrate on gaining her degree full time.

Thoughts of Martin plagued her night and day. Whatever his feelings for her, she could not allow him to continue to think her accident was in any way his fault. But how could she face him now, after all that had happened? Another day slipped by, then two. She knew she could not leave it any longer, but it was then, her mind made up, that she realised she had no idea how to find Martin, whereabouts in Devon his farm was located. The only contact number she had ever known was a mysterious answering service in London. Damian would know how to find him, she reasoned. She would stop in Dorset on her way down.

As the sun rose on another balmy June day, and before she could change her mind, Rebecca threw some things into an overnight bag, scribbled a brief note to Caroline, locked up the bungalow and set off.

"This is becoming a habit," Damian teased when he opened the door to her later that day. His smile faded and he frowned at her. "Is anything the matter? You look terrible."

"Thanks," she riposted with a grimace as she followed him inside the cottage and joined Jo in the living-room.

She was nervous, she admitted to herself a short while later as she sat with them drinking coffee. How could she explain why she wanted Martin's address? She had not so much as mentioned his name for three years, so they were bound to think it odd. Troubled, she set down her cup and saucer on the occasional table and walked across the room to look out at the riot of colour in the old-fashioned cottage garden.

"What's wrong, Rebecca?" Damian asked after a moment. "You've been strange since you arrived."

"I'm sorry, I just have a lot on my mind," she improvised with a brief smile.

Jo threw her a speculative glance. "I notice you're not wearing your ring."

"No." Rebecca glanced down at her bare finger. "I've decided I am not going to marry Tim," she explained, then frowned as a look of relief crossed her brother's face. "You seem pleased."

Damian gave an apologetic shrug. "I didn't think he was right for you."

"You never said anything."

"The most important thing to me is your happiness," he told her simply. "It's your life, Rebecca, and your decision how you choose to live it."

With a heavy sigh, she went back to her chair and sat down. "You may as well know that I've resigned from my job as well. I'm impatient to finish my degree, to be doing what I've always wanted, and I think I can manage financially now if I study full time."

"Good." Her brother smiled.

"A great idea," Jo agreed, "but you don't look very happy about it."

"Of course I am! The job was only intended as a stop-gap when I was unable to do anything else. It's time I moved on."

Jo sat back, a thoughtful expression on her face. "Why did you change your mind about marrying Tim?"

"I realised then it wasn't the right thing for me to do," Rebecca responded, fidgeting uncomfortably.

"Why?" Jo pressed, helping herself to a biscuit from a plate on the table.

Rebecca shrugged and tried to suppress the colour that threatened to stain her cheeks. "We weren't as compatible as I thought. We wanted different things."

"And have these 'different things' got anything to do with Martin?"

"What? I don't — "

"Jo!" Damian rebuked, cutting across his sister's stammered bemusement. "Leave it."

Rebecca looked from one to the other in puzzlement. "Leave what?" she asked, her frown deepening as they ignored her, seemingly intent on a silent battle of wills.

"I told you not to interfere," Damian chided his wife.

Jo waved her hand dismissively. "I am not going to stand on the sidelines any more, and I don't think you should either."

"Jo!"

"No, Damian, they are both making a mess of their lives, and you go around like a bear with a sore head whenever you see or talk to one or other of them. It's time to put a stop to this nonsense."

"What is going on?" Rebecca

demanded crossly as she rose to her feet. "Put a stop to what?"

Damian glanced at Jo for a long moment, then sighed. "Oh, all right," he agreed, dragging his fingers through his hair. "Sit down, Rebecca."

Rebecca did as she was told with reluctance. "I don't understand," she complained.

"Has this anything to do with Martin or not?" Damian asked at length.

"In a way." Rebecca looked down at her hands clasped tightly in her lap, rather bewildered at the turn of events, that Damian and Jo had zeroed in to the heart of the matter with such accuracy. "But — "

"You love him, don't you, Rebecca?" Jo interjected softly, ignoring her husband's exasperated sigh.

She felt the colour drain from her face, then reheat it in a rush. About to deny it, she took one look at the sympathetic understanding on Jo's face and her wall of pretence crumbled. She bit back a sting of tears. "Yes."

"Then why are you so stupid? What on earth is the problem between you?" Damian exploded as he jumped to his feet and paced about the room. "Jo is right. This has gone on long enough. Damn!" He muttered, almost to himself, "I wish I'd never said anything to him now."

Rebecca's eyes narrowed. "What do you mean?"

"You were so young, so naïve, even at eighteen, and in many ways you were dependent on me as a father-figure. I knew you had a crush on Martin, and I was worried you would mistake those feelings, and transfer that dependency on to him."

"Are you saying you warned him off?" she demanded incredulously.

"No, it wasn't like that, and Martin, well, it was nothing he didn't know already. I didn't want to hurt you. I was trying to be careful with your feelings," he defended. "I thought I was right, that it had been a teenage thing and you were over it. After the wedding, the accident, you never mentioned him any more — "

"Yes, the wedding, the accident," she said unevenly and drew in a shaky breath. "I had a fight with Martin after your wedding, I did . . . Well, the details don't matter now. But with that, and Mum and Dad, and you, my head was so messed up and confused, and I was so preoccupied, that I left the graveyard and stepped into the road without looking, and the bus — "

"You never told me this," Damian broke in, his face white. "Oh, Lord, Rebecca!"

"I didn't do it on purpose. And the last thing I was going to do was tell you what an idiot I had been, what I had done. If I never mentioned Martin, it was through embarrassment and shame — and he had made the situation between us perfectly clear," she added with another flash of pain at the memory. "Besides, he was off on another of his little jaunts. He's never really cared a fig about me."

Damian shook his head. "There are things you don't know."

"What things?"

"It's not my place to say. This is between the two of you, and you must ask him what you want to know. But go easy on him, Rebecca. The last three years have not exactly been a barrel of laughs for him, either."

"What do you mean?" she queried in confusion, her head buzzing with thoughts and questions.

Damian sat forward in his chair and took her hand in his. "I care about you both, Rebecca, but I will not take sides in this ridiculous cold war between you. I will not be played off one against the other. I've kept out of it until now, but you both drive me mad with your stubborn pride." He stopped and chose his words with care. "Now Martin is settled, and you've made new decisions, it's time you sorted things out. Someone has to make the first move. Rebecca," he continued, his eyes serious as he looked into her own. "Are you prepared to take the chance?"

Rebecca licked her lips, her nerves taut as she looked at the two caring, earnest faces before her. Then she nodded, her voice husky when she spoke.

"I'll try."

Before she had time to draw breath, she was in her car once more, and armed with detailed directions from Damian, she was sent with encouraging waves on her way to Devon. She see-sawed between anticipation and apprehension. Despite her brother's assurances, she could not believe Martin would welcome this unexpected visit. But, if nothing else, she had to swallow her pride, clear the air between them.

He may not accept her apology, she worried. She had said some awful things to him, allowed him to believe she blamed him for her accident. He may hate her for what she had done. A shiver ran through her. Was she doing the right thing? Had she been foolish to burn so many bridges behind her without testing the turbulence of the waters ahead?

She cut across the country roads before crossing the motorway and skirting the Exmoor National Park. As she reached Devon, a light rain began to fall, and the late afternoon sky turned overcast. She switched on the windscreen wipers and consulted the directions once more. According to Damian, the farm was located some way from the nearest village and was in an isolated spot on the edge of the Park. It took her ages to find the place. When at last she found the track, half-hidden by hedges, she stopped the car, tired, hungry and so nervous she didn't think she would find the courage to go on.

The cloud had lifted and brought with it the return of the sun. While she sat, gathering mental strength, she let out a slow whistle as she looked at the farm nestled in the valley below her.

"Wow!"

It was bigger than she had expected, more ordered, impressive. When Martin had mentioned his parents' old place, she had anticipated more of a smallholding, not dilapidated exactly, but run down, allowed to lie fallow.

Instead, the fields rolled gently before her, interspersed with small woods and copses, and a broad stream bisected the heart of the valley. She could pick out the house, with a range of stables and a barn and other outbuildings behind. Beyond them, several horses grazed in well-fenced, green paddocks, lush with grass. A bright-red tractor pulling a trailer laden with hay bales was moving slowly down a track towards the buildings. Her heart thumped as she strained her eyes to see if it was Martin behind the wheel. She couldn't tell.

Her nerves almost overcame her, and it took all her determination to put the car in gear and drive on. She opened the entrance gate, careful to close it securely behind her, and finally pulled up in front of the house. It was a beautiful building — mellow stone, long and low, and it had a warmth, a permanence that reached out to embrace her as she looked at it. She took a deep breath and rang the doorbell before she lost courage. There was no reply.

The noise of the tractor's engine grew louder, then spluttered to a stop. Rebecca followed a stone path that wound round behind the house, past a pond where a few ducks paddled and a weeping willow trailed its fronds in the water, through a gate beside a handsome kitchen garden and into the farmyard. The tractor, now minus its trailer, was parked in an open-fronted building, and a balding, middle-aged man alighted.

"Good-afternoon," Rebecca called as she walked towards him.

"Miss." He gave her a cursory glance up and down, then turned to extract a holdall from the cab of the tractor. "What would you be wanting?"

"Could you tell me where Mr Reid is, please?"

"Not selling anything, are you?"

"No, I just want to talk to him."

"He's a busy man, miss." The crusty farmer sniffed. "He don't like to be bothered."

"I won't keep him long." Rebecca smiled, amused at his suspicious protectiveness.

He scratched his head and stared at her again. "Reckon he'd be in the barn."

"Thank you for your help."

As she neared the barn, her steps faltered. Was she doing the right thing, she wondered for the hundredth time. What if . . . ?

Her chin lifted resolutely, her hands clenched into fists. Now was not the time for last-minute doubts, she told herself sternly. She flicked some stray strands of hair back from her face, smoothed down her powder-blue shirt, then thrust her hands into the pockets of the black jeans as she stepped through the door.

After the light outside, it took a moment for her eyes to adjust to the shadow in the barn. She heard the sound of voices, and a prickle of awareness ran up her spine as she recognised Martin's husky timbre. The barn was long and narrow, and at one end, a stocky teenager stood on a pile of hay bales. Martin, she saw, was on the laden trailer she had seen, tossing the bales up to his helper as if they were no more than loaves of bread.

Rebecca moved forwards, her footsteps silent on the soft, dirt floor. Outside, a bantam crowed, and the suddenness of the noise made her jump. As she went closer, she could see that Martin was stripped to the waist, perspiration glistening on his tanned flesh, his muscles rippling as he tossed up another bale.

She halted in shock at the sight of his back, her pulse racing. It was criss-crossed with scars, the marks of the welts fading but still angry against his sunkissed skin. She pressed a hand to her mouth, a frisson running down her spine, chilling her. What on earth had happened to him?

With an effort, she pulled herself together and took another few steps towards them. The youngster saw her and murmured something she could not catch to Martin. He turned and looked at her, and just for a moment, she thought she saw surprise, even pleasure in his eyes, before shutters dropped down to mask his expression. He rubbed a gloved hand across his damp forehead, then turned back to the young man who looked on with interest.

"Take a break, Johnny. We'll finish this later."

"Sure thing, boss." He grinned and climbed down from the stack before he left with a curious backwards glance.

Martin jumped down from the trailer, pulled off his gloves, and reached for his sleeveless, black T-shirt. He kept his back from her as he pulled it on, then walked towards her. For a moment, he looked at her in silence, and every nerve in her body was tense, vibrantly aware of him. Then, his gaze released hers and he stepped past her towards the door.

"You'd better come up to the house."

THE frosty reception did nothing to calm Rebecca's nerves, but she was determined to see this through. During the hard times of the last three years, she had found a strength of character she had not known she possessed. She would not allow her resolve to weaken now. This was too important.

She followed a pace behind as Martin led the way back across the yard to the rear of the house. He pushed open the door and led her into a spacious, stone-flagged kitchen, which was exactly how she had always imagined a proper farmhouse kitchen should be — the aged, pine table and chairs, the fireplace, the range with bunches of herbs and flowers hanging above to dry.

An old Labrador lay in front of

the range, and Rebecca watched in fascination as Martin's face softened and he stooped to pat the dog. Its tail thumped contentedly on the floor. For a brief moment, she envied the dog its place in Martin's affections, envied the gentle, tender way he looked at it, and the smooth caress of his hand.

Martin glanced at her as he stood up, his gaze hooded, his face aloof once more, she felt a tinge of colour stain her cheeks at the direction of her thoughts.

"Would you like some tea?"

"Yes, please," Rebecca responded to his painfully polite hospitality.

She welcomed the breathing space. It was always difficult in Martin's presence to concentrate her mind on what she wanted to say, so powerful was her awareness of him. She watched as he filled the kettle, set it on the range, then fetch the tea and milk, and take cups and saucers from the ancient dresser.

"Sit down," he invited, a gruffness in his voice.

"Thanks."

The legs of the chair scraped noisily on the stone floor. She sat down, and realised she now felt at a disadvantage, as if the slight gesture of submission had somehow given him control of the situation. She clasped her hands in her lap, tension building inside her as the silence stretched between them.

Rebecca dragged her gaze away, but after a brief sweep around the room, it automatically returned to him and found him watching her. His hair was tousled with a few stray wisps of hay. He was thinner and beneath the healthy tan, his face was drawn and tired. A muscle pulsed along his jaw which was dark with the shadow of stubble, and gave him a brooding appearance.

He was closed off from her, unapproachable — not that she could blame him after what she had done. The task ahead daunted her. Once a fool, always a fool?

Uncertain, Rebecca bit her lip, and watched from beneath her lashes as

Martin poured boiling water into the teapot. Her gaze followed every movement of his hands, the play of muscles up his bare arms, and she had to swallow down a rush of love and desire and mask her expression as he turned to her and handed her a steaming cup.

"Thank you."

Martin leaned against the range, his cup cradled in his hands as he looked at her, his eyes grey and indecipherable. "Why have you come?"

"I — " She struggled to compose herself, unsettled by his grim expression and implacable tone. "Martin, I — "

He cut across her stumbling hesitancy as he set his half-cup down on the table with a bang. "While you make up your mind what you are doing here, I'll go and change."

Left alone, she cursed her indecisiveness. She heard him take the stairs two at a time, and then his footsteps on the upstairs landing. Rebecca sipped the tea to revive her flagging spirits.

She had known this would not be easy, but Martin's reaction only made things more difficult for her. Coming here had been a gamble, and one she was determined not to lose.

Rebecca squared her shoulders, left her cup beside his on the table, and set off upstairs to find him. She walked quietly along the corridor and glanced through two open doors before she came to a large bathroom and found him.

He had changed into clean jeans, and now, unaware of her presence, he leaned on the pastel blue basin, his head bent. When she stepped forward, he raised his head, and as their gazes met in the mirror, she was stunned by the flash of naked anguish on his face before he masked it. She raised her hand and lightly began to trace the marks on his back.

Close to, under the artificial light, the scars were not as fresh as she had first thought, but were worse than she expected. Tears welled in her eyes and were reflected in the shake of her voice. "What happened?"

Martin spun away from her touch and ignored the question. He pulled on a navy T-shirt and brushed past her, leaving her with no option but to follow him back to the kitchen. When she arrived, he was filling the dog's water bowl.

"What is it you want, Rebecca?" he asked, his tone harsh and distant.

"To talk. Please," she insisted as he turned from her. "There are things I need to say."

He hesitated, his body tense, and Rebecca held her breath until he sat down with a brief nod of his head. "All right."

She let out a soft sigh of relief and joined him at the table. "It was very wrong of me to let you think, even for a moment, that I blamed you for the accident. That is not true. I'm sorry," she finished on a whisper.

"Have you any idea how I felt believing I was in any way responsible?"

he asked, the softness of his voice unable to hide his anger and hurt.

"I'm sorry. It honestly was not done with intent," she apologised again, wilting under his stormy grey stare. "It was an accident, pure and simple. When we talked that day and you said the words out loud, I realised I had been using it as an excuse. It was easier to blame someone else than accept that any fault was mine and mine alone."

Martin sat back in the chair and folded his arms across his chest. "You were upset, angry with me."

"I was confused about a lot of things, not only you," she assured him earnestly. "My parents, the wedding, my exams . . . it was an emotional time for me. None of which changes the fact that I stepped out into the road without looking. A four year old knows better than that."

As she watched, his eyes appeared to pass from grey through indigo back to blue as he thought over what she had said. She curled her hands into fists, her nails carving crescents in her palms.

"These headaches, the weakness in your leg, the pills, are they all legacies of the accident?"

"Yes."

His eyes held a troubled expression as he stared at her, and his voice was husky, unsteady. "Tell me about it."

Rebecca swallowed against the vivid rush of memories and rose to her feet to walk to the window. "When I looked up and saw the bus bearing down on me, I thought, this is it. I'm going to die."

At his sharp intake of breath, she turned to look at him. His eyes were closed, hiding his thoughts from her, but there was a pallor beneath the tan of his face.

"I was in a coma for a while," she continued, returning her unseeing gaze to the vegetable garden. "It took a while to track down Damian and Jo in Canada . . . I was conscious again by the time they returned."

All she had been able to think of from that moment on was working through each painful second, each minute, hour, day, week.

"How long were you in hospital?"

"Weeks," Rebecca told him and tried to ignore the weary desolation in his voice. "It took a long time to heal — longer to make my leg function and to learn to walk again."

She thought of the months of physiotherapy, of the struggle, the fear, the tears of frustration at the painful slowness of her progress.

"The nurses said I asked for you," she confided, angry at the wobble in her voice. "They left messages with your answering service."

"And I didn't come. You thought I didn't care?"

The sympathetic understanding in his voice tore at her heart, and she forced away a sting of tears. "It doesn't matter now."

"Of course it matters!" Martin swore under his breath. "Come and sit down," he instructed, waiting until she complied. He reached out a hand and cupped her chin, forcing her head up. "Look at me. I left the country within hours of leaving your house. The messages never reached me. Had I known, had I been here, I promise you I would have come."

Rebecca was held entranced by his deep blue gaze, the way the touch of his fingers seemed to brand her skin. Disconcerted, she sat back, breaking the contact.

"Tell me what happened then."

"The house was sold. I couldn't manage the stairs for a long time, and besides, I needed the money."

"Damian — "

"Damian and Jo did all they could, but they were in Dorset by then, and only had his doctor's salary. I was not going to take from them," she refuted hotly. "The house was left to us jointly, we each had our share, and I was able to manage."

Martin sighed deeply. "So that's why

you gave up university."

"Yes. Also, I needed some kind of income. It was my physiotherapist, of all people, who accidentally uncovered a talent for figures. He had a friend who was an accountant, and between them they found me this job which enabled me to work from home until I was strong enough to go to the office full time."

The job had not only provided a much-needed salary, Rebecca admitted to herself, but had helped her find some self-respect. Caroline, along with Damian and Jo, had been there for her all the way with supporting encouragement, but the biggest boost to her morale came when she could begin doing things for herself, could at least pay her own way, regain her independence.

"I'm surprised Damian didn't mention this," she went on and shot him a curious glance.

"You and me both, I was furious with him when I found out from you ... like that." He smiled, but it was a grim attempt and did not reach his eyes. It was his turn to rise to his feet and move away from her. "Damian said he had not anticipated us meeting again when we did, or he would have said something. Thank you for telling me now. Why did you?"

Rebecca licked her lips, nervous as she was subjected to an intense, penetrating stare. "I felt I owed it to you, I — "

"Of course," he interrupted, his voice stony, his eyes turning slate grey once more before he hooded them. He moved to the back door and pulled on a pair of boots. "Excuse me, I have to see to the horses."

"Can I come?"

He hesitated for an instant, not looking at her, then he nodded with evident reluctance. "If you like."

Rebecca suffered an attack of anxiety as she rose from the table and joined him. Why had he withdrawn from her, reverted to being cool and enigmatic?

For a brief moment there, she had almost allowed herself to believe he may care something for her after all. Had she made another foolish mistake? Loving him as she did left her open and vulnerable, and she knew all too well where that had led her once before.

She remained silent as they left the house, the Labrador following in their wake, and headed across the yard to the stables. Martin checked the deep straw bed in a large, empty box and filled the water bucket before he disappeared into a nearby feed room, shortly to return with a ration which he tipped into the food trough.

"I have to fetch him in," he explained in clipped tones as he took a lead rein from a hook outside the box and put a handful of nuts into a bucket.

The Labrador flopped down in the middle of the yard and watched with soulful eyes as Rebecca followed Martin down a broad path between the fields. Martin stopped at a paddock gate and banged the bucket against the post and rail fence. At the far end of the field, in the shadow of some trees, a horse raised its head and looked at them before it turned and broke into an uneven trot.

"Martin," she breathed involuntarily as the horse approached the gate.

"I know," he murmured in agreement, his eyes on the majestic animal, the proud carriage of its head before it halted in front of him and greedily attacked the bucket. Martin slipped the clasp of the lead rein on to the halter. "He's magnificent, isn't he?"

Rebecca ran her hand over the shining silk of the stallion's rich chestnut coat. "Where on earth did you find him?"

"Through Caroline. You know Caroline — she knows everyone who's anyone in horses."

"Did he race?" she asked, admiring the thoroughbred's athletic conformation.

"No, he's actually through an event line, Irish bred, but he broke down, tendon trouble . . . I expect you noticed his slight lameness?"

Rebecca nodded. "How old is he?"

"Only seven. My first stallion," he qualified, unable to keep a hint of pride from his voice as he rubbed the horse's ear. "He's as soppy as a lamb, too."

"What's his name?"

"He has a rather grand registered name, but he only answers to Ginger."

Rebecca smiled and traced the tiny white star between the kind, brown eyes.

"Hello, Ginger." She cast a sidelong glance at Martin as he opened the gate and led the horse through, careful to keep her voice light and teasing when she said, "You'd best watch out. I'm falling in love with him already!"

His mood changed with stunning abruptness, his body tensing, the expression in his eyes wintry as he shot her a glowering stare. "Don't play games with me, Rebecca."

"I'm not," she defended, stung by his snapping rebuke. But she was talking to his back. He strode off towards the stables, Ginger jig-jogging by his side, and she had to run to keep up with them.

He maintained a stony silence as he settled the horse in his comfortable stall then returned to the feed room. Confused and piqued, Rebecca sat on some sacks and trailed her fingers through the oats in the metal bin beside her, watching him measure out other feeds.

Was this barrier between them impenetrable, she wondered sadly as she looked at his grim, closed face. She was frightened to divulge too much, scared he would reject her again, and she didn't think she could stand the pain a second time. She just did not know where she stood with him. One moment he was chasing her, making her life so complicated and yet now, when she was prepared to talk, wanted to resolve the misunderstandings between them, he appeared determined to hold her at a distance. He was a difficult man to fathom.

"It's getting late," he said abruptly,

staring at her. "Are you staying with Damian and Jo, or have you found somewhere else?"

A chill crept across her skin and she closed her eyes. Clearly he did not want her here, but she had given no thoughts at all to her plans, where she would go, what she would do, if things did not work out as she hoped. She clenched her hands together in her lap. "I — " Her words choked off when he suddenly reached out and grasped her left wrist.

"Where's your ring? Don't tell me you've lost it in that bin?"

"No. I gave it back to Tim," she admitted, her gaze trapped as he looked at her and some of the coldness left his eyes causing her stomach to knot. "You were right. So was Caroline — I didn't love him. He has been a good friend, but I agreed to marry him for all the wrong reasons."

Martin released her hand and picked up four of the five buckets he had readied. He nodded towards the other one. "Will you carry that for me?"

"Of course."

Still wary of his constraint, she walked with him to a separate range of loose boxes that housed the mares away from the stallion. Some of the harshness had vanished from his expression as he glanced at her before he opened the first door, patted a neat, bay mare, then set down a bucket.

"So, what are you going to do now?"

"I've given up my job, and I'm going to finish my degree at university."

He raised one dark eyebrow and smiled faintly. "Good for you."

"I was offered a place three years ago," she elaborated, warmed by the approval in his voice. "If I explain the circumstances, I may still be able to go."

"Which university is that?"

She swallowed and met his gaze as he closed the second stable door.

"Exeter."

"Not far from here."

"I know."

His gaze intensified, turned blue, locked with hers, and an unwanted flush heated her cheeks. The chestnut mare in the box outside which they stood kicked against the door impatiently and broke the electric atmosphere. As Martin turned away reluctantly, Rebecca sucked some much needed air into her lungs, her pulse racing.

She paid scant attention to the fourth mare as she was engrossed in watching Martin. He was gentle and sure with the horses; she loved his grace and economy of movement, the way his muscles flexed. She loved to study his face, following the strong line of his jaw, the sensuous curve of his mouth, those amazing, chameleon-like eyes that changed through a range of colours with his mood, eyes that . . .

Her inspection halted and she took an involuntary step backwards, smothering a gasp. Those eyes were watching her watching him. Nerves fraught, her tongue moistened her lips in an unconscious gesture that caused his gaze to drop to her mouth before he raised it again, his eyes hooded, and deep blue.

"Don't look at me like that," he instructed huskily, his eyes closing, shutting her off from him. "Not if you don't — "

His pause stretched her already tense nerves. "If I don't what?"

"It doesn't matter. Forget it."

Rebecca drew in a ragged breath. "Martin — " She reached out a hand towards him but he evaded her.

"You made things plain enough, Rebecca. I'm thankful you've explained about your accident, glad about your plans for your degree. Let's leave it at that, shall we?" He dragged his hands through the thickness of his hair then reached for the bucket she held. "I'll take that."

As his hand closed around the handle, her own maintained its grip. She had seen a flash of vulnerability in his eyes that amazed her and she was not about to give up, not now that there was a reason for hope.

"I haven't finished all I came to say," she told him with a smile, surprised at the calmness in her voice.

"All right," he allowed after a quick glance round the yard. "But this isn't the place. I have to finish the horses, then we'll talk."

Rebecca surrendered the bucket which he promptly put down outside a small barn before he set off to check a group of horses in a nearby paddock. She leaned on the fence and watched him. Her lungs full of the clear, pure valley air, she was suddenly overwhelmed by a sense of belonging, as if she had been born to be here, with him . . . as if she had come home.

When he returned, she fell in step beside him. "It's so beautiful here."

"Thank you. I love it."

"I'm not surprised. I could stay here for ever."

Rebecca heard his sharp intake of breath and realised what she had said.

Her gaze flew to his face in time to catch a dark look of longing he failed to mask that set her body tingling in excitement. Her flesh burned as he took her hand in his.

"I want to show you something," he said after a timeless pause, and gave her a secret smile. "Come with me."

Rebecca's fingers twined with his of their own accord, enjoying the feel of his warm skin against her own. Love for him swelled inside her. It had to be all right between them, she told herself. How could it feel so wonderful otherwise?

"When I came back before Christmas, I bought my first mare," Martin told her as he picked up the bucket again and opened the door of the small barn. "It was my new start . . . hope for a future."

She looked at him quizzically, sensing a deep hurt and bitterness beneath his words. "How do you mean?"

"I'd had a rough time," he confided, a reserve in his tone. He tugged on her hand and drew her inside. "This way. The mare I bought was already in foal. He was born at the end of March. His mum cut her leg, so I've had them in for a couple of days."

A grey mare stood in one corner, and she looked at them, her ears pricked as they approached and Martin tipped her feed into a trough. In the straw beside her lay a dark bundle, a brown colt, all long legs, with a frizzy mane and squat tail. The bundle moved, the small, intelligent head lifting to stare at them, the soft-brown eyes full of mischievous curiosity before he flopped down sleepily again.

Rebecca laughed and watched him for a moment before she turned to find Martin sitting on the other side of the barn on some bales of straw. His expression was pensive as he leaned back, uncertain as he watched her. She walked across to join him, her fingers reaching out to brush a few strands of hair from his forehead. He caught her hand in his and held it. A muscle pulsed along the shadowed line of his jaw.

"You said you wanted to talk," he reminded her.

She sat beside him, sorry when he released her hand. "I thought I hated you for the way you rejected me, but seeing you again, it made me realise that nothing had changed. I'm still in love with you — I always have been."

"I'm not a child. I know what I feel. No, don't," she went on when he moved to interrupt, his words three years ago coming clearly to her mind. "I remember what you said, all of it. I was so humiliated — "

"Stop." He turned to her, and his fingers brushed across her lips, silencing her more effectively than anything else. "I didn't want to hurt you, but — "

Rebecca met his gaze as he paused. "But what?"

"You have to understand. I knew you had a crush on me, and I should have done more to discourage you. Why do you think I always tried to keep myself at a distance? You were so trusting, so vulnerable."

She flushed with embarrassment as she recalled her childish pursuit of him.

"After the wedding — " Her voice trailed off as he recaptured her hand.

"Yes, the wedding. Becky, I was responsible for you. You were so innocent, damn it, barely more than a schoolgirl, and your brother was my best friend. He trusted me. Besides, you had no idea what you were doing."

"I did," she protested heatedly.

Martin's fingers tightened on hers when she would have pulled away. "No you thought you loved me, but you had always been so studious with little experience of life for all your eighteen years. You needed time to grow."

"There's no need to make me sound so boring," she complained with a snap of petulance, annoyed when he grinned suddenly, unrepentant. "I may not have had much experience, but I always wanted you."

"I did what I thought was right. I was going away in a matter of hours, couldn't have protected you — I was not about to give in and leave you with the consequences. I didn't think I'd be away so long, nor that you would take what I said so much to heart. I'm sorry."

"So why did you kiss me like that?" she asked, warm even now at the thought of his lips on hers.

Martin's gaze slid away. "My intention was to frighten you into realising that you couldn't handle what you were asking for. It just got out of hand. I didn't mean to hurt you, but I had to put a stop to it."

"I know, you said. And it's not as if you even liked me really." She cursed the betraying wobble in her voice and raised her chin bravely.

"Oh, Becky, that's not true." He dragged his fingers through his hair and gave a wry laugh. "You still don't understand, do you? You have no idea what I'm telling you."

Eyes wide, she stared at him. "What are you telling me?"

"I was in deep trouble with you, Becky. I cared about you more than I thought possible, more than I knew was wise, and it scared the hell out of me. God help me, I wanted you," he told her roughly, shocking her, sending excitement coursing through her. "I wanted to take what you were offering, but I couldn't, for all the reasons I said, because it wouldn't have been right for you . . . because it would never have been enough. No, don't," he said as she moved instinctively into his arms. "If I kiss you now, I won't be able to think straight. Where was I?"

"You said something about it not being enough," she reminded him with a glow of pleasure.

"Yes." He pulled her head down against his shoulder and she slid her arms around him. "I thought I would be back in a couple of months and that the separation would give us both time to think. Then, when I came back, we could talk, see where we went from there. Your accident was obviously an unforeseen disaster, and so was the fact that my trip would go so badly wrong."

She glanced up at him in confusion. "What can go wrong in the Civil Service?"

"I wasn't in the CS."

"But you said — "

Martin shook his head. "No, you always assumed that and I let you, It was easier that way. I did work for the government, but I can't tell you how or why or what I did. I'm sorry."

"So what happened?" she asked in surprise, a flutter of alarm in her chest.

"It's a long story."

At the troubled weariness in his voice, she pushed against him and sat back so she could look at him. "I have time," she said softly. "Please?"

"Three of us were sent to Central America . . . false passports, assumed names, gathering and feeding intelligence to a particular faction."

"What went wrong?" she prompted when he paused.

Martin's eyes clouded and his fingers tightened their grip on hers. "We had been there nearly two months, were just about due to come home, when there was a coup. The place was in turmoil. We couldn't get out and, well, we were in the wrong place at the wrong time. We were interrogated, found guilty of being enemies of the state, and chucked in jail."

"Martin, no!" Shock tightened her nerves as she tried to push a rush of images of his interrogation and imprisonment from her mind. "Why didn't anyone help you?"

"That's one of the drawbacks of the job," he said, his voice hard. "A fact of life we were all aware of. If things go wrong, you are on your own — no official connection with the government."

Rebecca gave an angry exclamation of disgust. "They can't just forget you if you're in trouble," she declared hotly. "What did you do?"

"What we were trained to do — make the best of it."

She sensed there was much he was not telling her and shivered at the thought of what he must have been through. "It must have been dreadful."

"Yeah. I've spent a better couple of years, I can tell you that. There were times I felt like giving up, we all did. We had no idea how long we might be there, if we'd ever get out alive, but I thought of home, of this place — of you."

The thought of him in danger, his life threatened, terrified her. "Oh, God, if anything had happened to you." She buried her face against his chest with a stifled sob.

He tipped her chin up with a finger and smiled. "Don't worry, it's over, and I'm returned in one piece, near enough."

"Your back, you — "

"Let's just say none of us was left

in any doubt what would happen if we stepped out of line."

Tears stung her eyes. Even the thought of what could have happened to him made her feel ill. "How did you get out?"

"There was a revolution, the right side this time, and suddenly, we were free to leave. We didn't stop to ask questions. We arrived back in England at the end of November."

"I hope you told them where they could stick their job."

A smile tugged his mouth at the vehemence in her voice. "Not in precisely those words, but yes, I'm a free man now, in more ways than one."

"And then you came here?"

"Yes." His hand slid into her hair. "I was pretty messed up, physically and emotionally. It's taken a few months to get my head together and recuperate, and the activity of setting the farm back on its feet, of planning for the horses, was excellent therapy as I built up my strength."

Rebecca expelled a long breath and shifted closer to him. "Did Damian know any of this?"

"Most of it. I always give him as a contact — he's the closest thing to family I have," Martin admitted. "He heard things had gone wrong, but he didn't know where I was or what was happening."

How had her brother coped all the time, worrying about his best friend on top of his anxiety about her own accident? She felt dreadful for thinking as she had about Martin all this time when he had been suffering a hell of his own.

"I didn't want him telling you, letting you know I was back," he continued, twisting some of her hair through his fingers. "You don't know how much I wanted to see you, but I couldn't, not until I had straightened myself out."

"It's all right."

"No, it isn't, I had planned to move back into your life gently, but you turned up at Damian's and Jo's unexpectedly." His smile was rueful. "You caught me unprepared."

Rebecca made a face at him. "You aren't the only one. I had the shock of my life. I'm sorry I've been so horrible. I was so wrapped up in myself, confused, wanting to hate you for past hurts, protect myself because I was still attracted to you."

"You could have fooled me! I didn't realise how much damage I had done that night, and when I saw how much animosity remained. When I discovered you were engaged . . . " He shrugged helplessly.

"Why didn't you tell me all this sooner?"

"The way you reacted when I was around — well, I believed that it was a crush you had on me after all, that you had grown out of it. I was devastated. You were pretty insistent you wanted nothing more to do with me."

"Not that you took much notice!" She smiled and met the intensity of his blue gaze. "I was frightened of you, of how you made me feel, and I was so confused. I never thought you could care for me, not after the things you said, so I thought you were just amusing yourself with me."

"No! Don't ever think that. It's just — " His fingers tightened in her hair, holding her face back so he could look at her. "When I thought you really were going to marry Tim, I had to try something drastic."

"I persuaded myself Tim was what I needed because he was everything you weren't. I was wrong. You are all I've ever needed."

"Oh, Becky," he groaned in exasperation. "We've wasted so much time."

He pulled her head to his, and at last their lips met. She was lost in the magic of his kiss as the touch of his jaw rubbed pleasurably against her skin. Her arms curled around his neck as he leaned back and pulled her with him into a soft pile of straw.

When he pulled back from her, she

moaned in protest, but as her eyes slowly opened and she looked up at him, she saw he was laughing. The colt, roused from his sleep, had given in to his mischievous nature. His soft nose was inches from her own as he stood over them and butted Martin out of the way. His mother looked on with martyred resignation as her son nibbled Rebecca's hair. Rebecca laughed as Martin sternly told the youngster off and pulled her to her feet.

"I think the house will be more private," he murmured against her ear. "I don't want any kind of audience when I detail my plans for you."

Warm with excited anticipation at the husky promises in his voice, they walked back to the house, his arm curving her possessively against his side.

"My big brother will want to know if your intentions are honourable, Mr Reid," she told him primly as he kicked the door shut and pulled her into his arms.

"Not at the moment they aren't,"

Martin answered with a rakish grin before he trailed a tantalising line of kisses down her neck. "But, if you think he'll come after me with a shotgun," he mouthed against the hollow of her throat, "perhaps I'd better marry you. It might be safer."

Rebecca's breath caught. "Is that supposed to be a proposal?"

"Mmm." He frowned as she pushed against him. "Stop distracting me."

"I haven't decided if I want to marry you."

"Really?" His hold tightened, his own eyes reflecting the teasing light in hers. "Then I shall just have to keep you here until you say yes."

Rebecca smiled and sank her fingers into the thickness of his hair.

"That's a pity."

"Why?"

"Because I won't say yes. I want to be kept here, with you . . . for always."

He groaned and buried his face in her hair. "I'm too old for you,

you know," he muttered, almost to himself, but loudly enough to rouse her temper.

"I do wish you'd stop harping on this silly age business. Eight years is nothing," she argued hotly.

"Have I told you how lovely you are when you're angry?"

Rebecca frowned crossly as she realised he was teasing her. Two could play that game! She schooled her features and affected an air of unconcern.

"Besides, I can always trade you in for a toy boy if you don't come up to scratch," she said, laughing as his eyes darkened with warning.

"I wouldn't advise you to try it!" She welcomed the pressure of his mouth on hers, the teasing gone. "I love you, Becky," he whispered, his voice thick with emotion. "And I'll spend the rest of our lives proving it."

As Rebecca was lost in the magic of his kiss once more, she knew their lives were just beginning. They had each been through a voyage of self-discovery, and each had overcome the trials they had faced. In doing so, they had come full circle. They had found each other . . . and had found love.

Foolish Heart

In memory of Kay
with love and affection

Sam was everything Jenny could want in a man — handsome, clever and charming, and she knew she could easily fall in love with him. But her heart had already been broken and she had vowed never to make the same mistake again.

1

JENNIFER WILSON drummed her fingers against the steering-wheel as the queue for the multi-storey carpark inched forward at a snail's pace. It was after one o'clock and she was already late.

She slipped the car back into first gear and edged closer to the entrance. Why had she agreed to brave the holiday traffic and bring her fifteen-year-old brother to Portsmouth?

A wry smile pulled the generous bow of her mouth. As soon as Peter had heard this particular naval ship would be in dock, he had twisted her round his little finger . . . as usual.

At last she reached the automatic barrier and she stabbed at the button of the ticket machine with an impatient finger. Then she drove up the ramps, searching each level for a vacant space.

The hunt increased her irritation. Finally, she located a departing car and deftly reversing into the space, grabbed her bag, locked up and walked briskly towards the stairs.

Once outside and back under the merciless July sun, Jennifer hurried through the arch beside the Victory Gate and made her way through the crowds to the souvenir shop.

After the brightness outside, her eyes took a moment to adjust as she scanned the interior for Peter's light brown hair. He was nowhere to be seen. Jennifer frowned and absently raised a hand to brush some damp tendrils of fair hair from her forehead.

Across the shop a tall, attractive man with sun-bleached hair leaned casually in the doorway that led through to the exhibition hall. He was wearing mirrored sunglasses that hid his eyes, and yet Jennifer could feel his gaze on her.

She sent him a cool, disinterested look and resumed her search for Peter. Out of the corner of her eye, she saw the man move from his position and begin to head in her direction. With an inward groan, she altered her course away from him.

Despite her obvious attempts to avoid him, the man blocked her path and forced her to stop. Annoyance clouded her grey eyes as she glanced up at him, only to find herself irritated further by the slow grin that spread across his face.

"Are you Jennifer Wilson?"

The warm huskiness of his voice shocked her almost as much as his question.

"Yes, I am. Who are you?"

"Peter asked me to watch out for you," he explained without immediately answering her own enquiry. His smile widened. "He won't be long."

"Thank you for letting me know. I'll wait for him," Jennifer dismissed the stranger. There was something about him that disturbed her. Turning away she went back to the doorway, grateful for the faint breeze she found there.

"My name is Sam. Sam Harper."

Jennifer suppressed a sigh but could not disguise the look of annoyance that crossed her face as she turned towards the man once more. She saw his outstretched hand and accepted the gesture automatically, displeased to find that his firm touch lingered longer than was necessary. Withdrawing her hand she stepped back.

"Thank you, Mr Harper. There is no need for you to wait," she assured him, her voice cool and, she hoped, fairly distant.

He watched her from behind those glasses, his head tilted to one side as his hand rose to touch the softness of her hair that fell in gentle curls to her shoulders.

"Your brother was wrong when he said you were pretty."

"Mr Harper," she began indignantly, her eyes sparkling as she pushed his hand away. "I — "

Jennifer closed her eyes and took a deep breath.

"Mr Harper, you have delivered your message, for which I have already thanked you. I have no wish to detain you any longer."

"What a pity!" He smiled that slow, easy smile. "A bit prickly today, aren't you?"

Jennifer opened her mouth to make a tart reply, but finding that nothing suitable came readily to mind, she snapped it shut.

He considered her for a moment.

"Pretty is the wrong adjective for you . . . it doesn't do you justice."

Jennifer had no wish to be pretty, or any other adjective he was thinking of for that matter. Why couldn't he just go away and leave her alone? Surely she had made it plain enough that she did not want to talk to him.

He moved to one side to allow a group of people to pass and Jennifer had the opportunity to study him for a moment.

He was dressed in a pair of faded jeans that moulded his long legs and his feet were encased in a pair of smart, comfortable-looking trainers. The plain, bright red shirt he wore was open at the neck revealing the strong column of his throat, and the short sleeves were rolled up an extra once or twice.

He was probably over six feet, she assessed, although it was difficult to tell in the confines of the shop. He looked lean and fit. His skin was tanned — perhaps too tanned for England in July, despite the intensity of the heatwave of the last couple of weeks.

What Jennifer was able to see of his face was very attractive. He had a straight nose, a firm, clean-shaven jaw, and a mouth that looked as if it often smiled.

His short, thick, blond hair was unruly and naturally streaked from the sun. His glasses hid his eyes and effectively prevented her from discovering their colour or reading their expression.

She wondered how her brother had met him, if he came from the ship

Peter had been so anxious to see. But somehow, Sam did not look like a sailor. Jennifer smiled to herself. What did a sailor look like?

Through the doorway she saw Peter as he crossed the wide road that led through the base to the jetties, museums and ships.

She stepped outside to greet him. In the distance, she could see the masts and rigging of HMS *Victory*, its black and yellow paintwork glinting in the sunshine.

"Sorry, Jen. Have you been waiting long?"

The lanky teenager smiled endearingly and, as usual, Jennifer was unable to remain annoyed at him for long.

"No. I was held up myself."

Peter glanced behind her.

"You've met Sam then?"

Jennifer nodded her head slightly in acknowledgement and hid a grimace. Hadn't she just!

"His brother is on the ship," Peter continued. "I met them both on board.

She is terrific, Jen! She sails in the morning. I wish I could be here to see it."

Jennifer smiled at the wistful tone in her brother's voice. It was Peter's dream to join the Navy, he was so besotted with the sea and all things nautical.

She hoped everything would work out for him, and if enthusiasm counted for anything, he would make it.

"I've asked Sam to have lunch with us," Peter informed her.

The smile left Jennifer's face. She knew she could not protest without being rude, and Peter obviously enjoyed Sam's company.

They had clearly developed a rapport despite the difference in age. Sam, she decided, must be at least thirty, although she realised it was quite difficult to tell.

They decided to have lunch at a nearby pub, and sat outside at a wooden table, partly shaded by a large, colourful umbrella. Jennifer sipped her ice-cold drink, idly watching the ferries and small boats that went busily to and fro in the harbour.

While they ate their sandwiches, Jennifer found herself wondering about Sam. She was beginning to think far too much about him, she chided herself, and was impatient for lunch to be over so they could go their separate ways.

She had promised Peter she would join him for a boat trip round the harbour that afternoon and, to her horror, she discovered that the invitation had been extended to Sam to join them for this as well.

"Peter, I am sure Mr Harper has other things to do. We have taken up enough of his time already," Jennifer finished pointedly.

"I'm looking forward to it," Sam assured her with an amused smile. "I had nothing else planned for the afternoon."

Jennifer rose from the table, wondering just why this man was making her so temperamental.

"Well, you two go and enjoy yourselves and I'll do some sketching."

"Jen, you promised."

Peter's protest was tinged with a faint trace of petulance and Jennifer bit her lip. How could she explain to her brother that Sam's presence was responsible for her ill humour and expect him to understand? She did not understand it herself.

"All right," she conceded, glad to see the smile back on Peter's face. She glanced across at Sam who grinned, making her fume. Infuriating man!

As they walked along the seafront to the jetty, Peter ran ahead to buy the tickets.

"Peter tells me you're an artist. What medium do you work in?" Sam enquired, breaking the silence that had lengthened between them.

"Oils mostly," Jennifer explained, a smile animating her features as she talked of the work she loved so much. "I paint landscapes, wildlife . . ."

"You do commissions?"

"Some, but not as many as I used to, unless the subject is interesting to me. I've given up painting family pets! I prefer to paint what I feel."

"You're very young to be making such a good living from your work."

Jennifer bristled. How many times had she heard that remark before?

"I am twenty-four, but I fail to see what age has to do with it. My work obviously speaks for itself, Mr Harper."

Sam raised his hands in mock surrender.

"It was an observation, not a criticism. Don't be so touchy."

Embarrassed by her uncharacteristic loss of temper, Jennifer refrained from further comment, relieved to see they were about to rejoin Peter.

After the boat had been tied up at the jetty and the previous passengers had disembarked, Jennifer stepped over the side and gratefully accepted the help offered by the ticket collector.

However, she still managed to slip

when she reached the bottom and was saved from falling by a firm arm grabbing her. As she was drawn against a masculine body, she spread her hands on a broad chest to steady herself and glanced up.

"Thank you."

"The pleasure was all mine!" Sam said, grinning down at her.

A tinge of colour washed Jennifer's cheeks and she pushed against him.

"I can manage fine on my own now."

"If you insist."

"I do," she stressed, stepping hastily away from him the instant he relaxed his hold.

They sat in the stern gathering as much of the cooling breeze as they could. Jennifer loved the sun and welcomed long, dry summers, but it was always a while before she became accustomed to the heat.

Fishing in her canvas bag, she found a green ribbon that matched her sundress, and tied her hair back in a ponytail, savouring the feel of the cool air as it fanned her heated skin.

When she looked round, she discovered Sam watching her, a smile tugging at his mouth. Jennifer withdrew her gaze from her own reflection in his sunglasses and wished he would stop looking at her. It made her uncomfortable.

Despite the kindness of Mother Nature, she was neither vain nor complacent about her looks. She was far more interested in people's personalities than the way they looked.

Nor was she unused to men looking at her ... it was just there was something about the way Sam looked that affected her.

As soon as the trip began, Peter started to point out all the noteworthy things they passed, and Jennifer smiled wryly at his enthusiasm.

She listened as Peter chattered incessantly to Sam and grudgingly admitted that the older man showed every interest and encouragement. She respected him for that.

The tour took them round the harbour, passing several warships and various places of historical interest. Craft of all shapes and sizes bustled about, and occasionally a helicopter whirred overhead.

Although it was a calm day, the movement of the boat, the heat and the vaguely oily fumes from the engine combined to make Jennifer feel queasy. She breathed a sigh of relief when the boat finally came to a halt at the jetty, anxious to be back on dry land.

"Are you all right?"

Jennifer nodded in response to Sam's query and reluctantly accepted the hand he offered to assist her up the steps. His touch was warm and firm . . . and it disturbed her. She broke the contact as soon as her feet hit the jetty.

"Thank you," she murmured politely, then offered a small shrug and a rueful smile. "I'm very much a landlubber, I'm afraid. Peter's love affair with boats does not run in the family!"

Jennifer instantly regretted her choice

of words as a teasing smile came to Sam's face. He raised a provocative eyebrow.

"What sort of love affair does interest you?"

He appeared to enjoy baiting her and Jennifer fumed as she clenched her hands into fists. She would not allow him to embarrass her. With a cool smile, she turned to Peter.

"I'll fetch the car while you say your goodbyes," she informed him, then gave her antagonist a brief nod of dismissal. "Mr Harper."

"Goodbyes are so final, don't you think?" he teased, clearly amused by her hostile attitude. "I hope we'll meet again."

"Most unlikely."

"We'll see," he countered with an enigmatic smile.

Jennifer walked away, inwardly muttering to herself. Did the man always have to have the last word? And his ego was colossal. He must think he was God's gift to women with his film star looks and his easy charm.

But it didn't affect her. She was immune to men . . . especially men like Sam Harper.

★ ★ ★

On the journey home to the outskirts of the Sussex town of Arundel, Peter talked of little else but his visit to the ship and meeting Sam. Jennifer's patience was stretched to the limit.

It was all she could do to refrain from snapping at him to be quiet about the hateful man. And if Peter seriously thought they were likely to see him again . . . She swallowed down a derisive exclamation.

To her irritation, Peter gave a detailed account of the day to the rest of the family at supper that evening. Jennifer's other brother, Mark, who was younger than her but older than Peter, and her parents listened with amusement.

Jennifer glowered at her youngest sibling and concentrated on her meal with studied care in an attempt to block out his chatter, until she thought her nerves would snap.

"Sam's a sports journalist," Peter explained.

"I've heard of him," Mark commented, helping himself to an extra large spoonful of mashed potato. "He's a really good writer, won the sports journalists' award a few times, I think. He wrote that book on the World Cup I got for my birthday."

"Have you still got it?" Peter looked up eagerly. "Can I borrow it?"

"Sure. It's on the bookshelf in . . . " Mark glanced across at Jennifer with a grin as Peter dashed from the table. He shrugged and added with quiet amusement, " . . . in my room!"

Jennifer grimaced as she heard Peter's footsteps on the upstairs landing, annoyed by his childish enthusiasm. What on earth was all the fuss about?

"He seems quite taken with this

man." Her mother smiled. "Did you meet him, Jen?"

"Mmm," she murmured non-committally.

"What was he like?" Ann Wilson persisted.

Jennifer fixed her gaze on her plate and shrugged.

"I didn't pay any attention." She was thankful that Peter returned and saved her from further comment.

"It lists the other books he's written here — I'll have to have a look in the library," Peter announced.

"Is that a photograph of him?" Eric Wilson asked, and Jennifer followed her father's gaze to the back cover of the book.

Peter turned it over and nodded.

"Yes. He's really nice, Mum. And he has a terrific sense of humour. You'd all like him."

Jennifer closed her eyes and counted to ten in an effort to control an angry outburst.

Oh, yes, he had a sense of humour,

all right, just terrific, she mused crossly. Arrogant, infuriating man.

If they didn't shut up about Mr Sam massive-ego, know-it-all Harper, she would scream!

She glanced up and flushed slightly when she met her father's questioning gaze.

Her mother took the book and studied the photograph.

"What a good-looking young man, and he has a lovely smile," she proclaimed, making Jennifer cringe. "You say you didn't talk to him much, Jen?"

"No."

"She was pretty rude to him really," Peter retorted.

"I was not!"

"You were, too," he insisted. "It was embarrassing for me, but Sam thought you were funny!"

Jennifer felt a tide of angry colour suffuse her face.

Aware of the speculative glances cast her way, she forced herself to smile and change the subject, asking Mark about the holiday he was taking with his friends.

This year they were cycling round Europe before the majority of them settled down back home and went to university in the autumn.

Satisfied she had successfully deflected the family's attention, she sat back and sipped the coffee her mother poured for her.

Before she went to bed that night, Jennifer spent an hour in her studio before going downstairs and out to the garden for some fresh air.

It had been hot under the slate roof of her attic studio. Now, in the cool of the summer evening, it was relaxing to sit for a while, watch the stars and savour the scent of the honeysuckle, jasmine and night-scented stock.

Over the next few days, life returned to normal, and Jennifer managed a smile at her uncharacteristic ill-humour.

The subject of Sam and the trip to

Portsmouth had been forgotten and Jennifer was content for it stay that way.

It was nothing to get worked up about, she chided herself as she set off for a day's sketching by the castle and in the park.

Mark had set off on his European adventure and Peter had plenty to occupy him with his friends during the holidays.

With her mother at her job in a local estate agents, and her father busy at his solicitors' practice in nearby Chichester, Jennifer was relieved to have some space to concentrate on her work.

Now, as she leaned back against a fallen log in the local park and made some sketches of the lake, she was annoyed to find that Sam's image refused to be banished from her mind.

Why the cursed man had provoked such a violent reaction from her she was still at a loss to work out. What annoyed her more now was to find herself absently committing his likeness to paper.

Impatient with herself, Jennifer packed her things and moved position to the other side of the lake.

Her paintings sold well, and her pen and ink sketches of the local area and its wildlife were always in demand and popular with the tourists. But her determination to concentrate was frustrated, and she finally succumbed and allowed her creative fingers free rein.

When she glanced at the pages in her sketchbook, she had to admit they were good. She had captured Sam in various poses, and was surprised and disturbed to discover she had paid him enough attention. An artist's habit, she excused herself.

The black and white photograph on the book Peter had produced had not solved the mystery about Sam's eyes. For goodness' sake, she rebuked herself, do stop thinking about the wretched man! Even if he was incredibly handsome, it meant nothing.

She had been down that road once before, and look where it had left her. Just forget him, she lectured herself. Forget him and settle down to some sensible work.

She had begun a sketch of the lake when a holiday-maker came to investigate. However much she hated to be interrupted, Jennifer was always friendly on these occasions, knowing people would remember her and her work. It was always worth taking the time and trouble to talk with them, to share her love and knowledge of the area.

The summer ahead would be a busy time. She would need to keep all her various outlets stocked with work, she had a couple of paintings to finish for clients, and she had to prepare for her annual summer exhibition.

Making the most of the light, and pleased by what she had eventually been able to accomplish, it was late when Jennifer arrived home for supper that evening.

She hurried indoors and dashed upstairs to deposit her equipment in her studio before she had a wash. Her mother hated her to arrive at the table covered with ink blotches and smudges!

After she had tidied herself and changed from her shorts and T-shirt into a brightly-patterned cotton dress, she went down to join the others for supper.

As she went through the dining-room door, she snatched off her headband to allow her fair hair to fall around her face, and was in the middle of apologising for her lateness when she halted, her mouth falling open in disbelief.

Sitting at the table was Sam Harper.

2

CONSCIOUS that everyone was looking at her, Jennifer pulled herself together and took her usual place at the table, disconcerted to find that Sam was seated opposite her.

He smiled as she sat down and she inclined her head in a brief but unwilling gesture of acknowledgement.

"You remember Sam, of course," her mother prompted as she handed Jennifer a serving dish.

"Of course." She struggled to control the grim reluctance in her tone. She would absolutely not look at him, Jennifer vowed. "Good evening, Mr Harper. This is a . . . surprise."

"A pleasant one, I hope."

She wanted to refute his statement but knew she could not under the circumstances — not with her parents and Peter hanging on every word. And surely they must sense the charge of tension that flowed back and forth across the width of the mahogany table between herself and Sam.

But the evident amusement in his voice when he had made his sly challenge had raised Jennifer's hackles. Must he always laugh at her? She met his gaze with the intention of registering her annoyance, and instead found herself transfixed by his eyes.

She had thought about them, hidden as they had been that first day behind those unsocial sunglasses he had worn. She had wondered about their colour, had expected blue, quite possibly green. They were neither. She had never seen eyes quite like them before. They were an unusual warm, spicy, reddish-brown colour, like ground cinnamon.

It took her a confused moment to realise those eyes were holding her stare. Embarrassed that he had caught her looking at him so intently, she returned her attention to the salad on her plate, but her appetite had deserted her.

Her mind buzzed. What on earth was Sam doing here? Jennifer experienced a sudden irrational wave of panic.

"Peter tells us you have a brother in the Navy," her father remarked, and Jennifer breathed a sigh of relief that Sam's attention was temporarily deflected from her.

"Yes, David is on the ship Peter was visiting," he responded and that faintly husky voice seemed to wrap around Jennifer, holding her captive. She tried to shake off the sensation as Sam continued.

"David is three years younger than me. Joining the Navy was the only thing he ever wanted to do, right from when he was tiny. Just like Peter here. It was the only dream he had."

"Then you know how it is!" Ann Wilson smiled. "Do you have any other family?"

"An older sister, Alison. She is married to a vet and they live in the Scottish Borders. My paternal grandparents are still alive," he added. "Grandpa is a Scot and they live in Edinburgh."

No parents, Jennifer thought, unable to switch off from what Sam was saying, despite telling herself she was not interested. As if he sensed what she was thinking, he glanced at her then back to her mother.

"My dad died when I was six. I don't remember very much about him. Mum raised us. She worked as a nursing sister while we were at school and saw us all started." He paused for a moment and Jennifer glanced up and met his gaze. "She died last year in an accident."

She felt a welling of sympathy at the sadness he had been unable to keep from his voice.

Theirs had been a close unit, she could tell, the same as her own family. She could not bear to imagine a time when neither of her parents would be there.

After a struggle, Jennifer wrested her gaze away again. She did not want to feel empathy with this man, less still to find that she liked him. It would be far safer to keep him at a distance.

Her mind troubled, Jennifer toyed with her food as Peter talked to Sam about his writing and the book on the World Cup.

She was not interested in sport, but still found herself listening to Sam, watching the changing expressions on his face, the way his lips moved when he talked. Annoyed with herself, she pushed her plate aside and took a sip of ice-cool water.

"Mark, our other son who is in Europe at the moment," her mother explained, "told us you had won the sports journalists' award several times."

Sam looked embarrassed, Jennifer realised with surprise as she watched him shrug.

"A couple of times, yes. I've been lucky that a few good stories have come my way."

After the meal, Jennifer helped Peter with the dishes and looked forward to the moment she could escape to her studio to mull over the turn of events.

Never in a million years had she expected Sam to honour his promise to Peter to keep in touch.

And however pleased she was for her brother, she still did not like Sam being here. He made her uncomfortable.

He had not come over as the egotistical villain she had branded him — at least not when he spoke of his work. Clearly he was successful and respected in what he did, but he chose not to brag about it.

And he loved his family, she could tell that by the tone of his voice. Which has nothing to do with anything, Jennifer rebuked herself, furious that despite her attempts to banish him, Sam had invaded her thoughts yet again.

"Sam and I are going to watch the county cricket in the castle grounds tomorrow," Peter informed her as he squirted an extra dash of washing-up liquid into the water.

"He's staying then?" Jennifer's heart sank as she contemplated the situation.

"Of course. He has a couple of weeks' holiday. It's a pity that I'm going on this trip with John."

"You've been looking forward to this adventure holiday for weeks," Jennifer reminded him with a touch of exasperation.

"I know, but if I was here, I could show Sam round." Peter cast her a sideways glance and grinned. "You'll have to take him out with you. It will make up for you being so rude to him!"

Jennifer ignored her brother's baiting, but her fingers tightened on the tea-towel in her hands.

"I doubt he will be in the area. I expect he just looked in to visit you." I hope, she added silently.

"Oh, no. Mum's invited him to stay with us. That's what I meant."

Her mouth dropped open in horrified amazement.

"What? You are joking?"

"What's wrong with him staying?"

"Well, he just can't, it's ridiculous. Why, we don't even know anything about him," she finished in desperation.

"What are you afraid I might do, Jenny, run off with the family silver?"

The sound of Sam's mocking voice had Jennifer spinning round, and the plate she was drying slipped from her fingers and smashed on the floor.

A blush rose up from her neck to her hairline in a hot tide of colour. Sam walked into the kitchen and took the scourer from Peter's hand.

"I'll finish helping with this," he told him. "You go and watch that programme you were anxious to see."

"Thanks, Sam."

Peter grinned and shot Jennifer a wink. She itched to give him a piece of her mind, but he dashed off and closed the door behind him.

Jennifer collected the dustpan and

brush and swept up the remains of the plate she had broken. A tense knot of apprehension settled in her stomach. Warily, she returned to her drying duties and allowed herself to be lulled into a false sense of security as the silence lengthened.

When the washing-up was finished, Sam leaned against the counter between her and the door and effectively blocked her only exit.

"So," he murmured with deceptive softness. "If it's not the safety of the family silver that's worrying you, what is?"

Jennifer cast a longing glance at the door. The words locked in her throat as she tried to speak.

"Maybe it is something more elemental that bothers you about my being here?"

"Such as?" she managed, disturbed by his closeness.

"Perhaps you are afraid that I'll eventually find a way past those prickles of yours." He smiled, but the expression in his eyes was watchful, searching. "Or are you more afraid still that you might want me to?"

"Don't be silly."

The denial was wrenched from her. The man was insufferable. What did he expect? She refused to be swayed by that easy charm and beguiling smile. Certainly not after what happened last time . . .

She closed her eyes and reined in her thoughts, but her head lifted in alarm when Sam took another step towards her.

Frozen, unable to move, she watched as he raised a hand and ran one finger down her cheek with agonising slowness. Her skin burned from his touch.

The telephone rang, but before she could use it as an excuse to escape, it stopped, and she knew someone had answered it in another part of the house.

Not to be diverted, Sam's finger slid beneath her chin and tipped her face up until her gaze met with his.

"What are you hiding from?" he asked softly.

"Nothing."

"I can see it in those anxious grey eyes of yours."

Jennifer pushed his arm away to free herself from the disturbing touch that seemed to rob her of the power to think.

"You're imagining things."

"Something has put that fear there, the doubt, wariness, distrust . . . " His gaze sharpened as he looked at her, then he added with devastating perceptiveness, "Or perhaps it's someone."

Stunned, Jennifer stared at him. How could he read her so easily, probe behind the very fabric of the defensive wall she had so recently erected for protection?

A shiver travelled up her spine. This man was dangerous.

She almost collapsed with relief when her mother pushed open the kitchen door and rescued her from the necessity of having to give a reply.

"All done?" She smiled. "Ian is on the phone, Jen. He wants a word before he flies out."

"Thank you."

Avoiding his gaze, Jennifer edged past Sam and could have hugged both Ian and her mother for their timely intrusion. Behind her, she heard her mother explaining to Sam.

"Ian is a photographer — an old family friend. He's off on a photo safari to The Gambia . . ."

The door swung closed and cut off all but the murmur of conversation. Jennifer sent up further grateful offers of thanks for her rescue and went to the extension in the living room to talk to Ian.

* * *

Peter kept Sam occupied over the next couple of days, and Jennifer was able to avoid meeting him apart from at supper. She found the meal a strain each evening, aware of Sam's gaze on her, his quiet speculation.

The uneasy feeling remained with her that she may not escape his clutches with such effectiveness a second time.

Then Peter left on his summer trip and, for a brief instant, Jennifer felt very alone, with him and Mark and Ian all gone.

After the events of recent weeks since the break-up of her last relationship, she felt cut off, adrift from her old crowd of friends. But, she asserted, she would try not to think about it. She would not allow Nigel and what he had done to continue to prey on her mind.

To her dismay, and thanks to her mother's interfering, however well-meant, Jennifer found herself stuck with Sam and forced to play reluctant tour guide.

"Are you sure you don't have better things to do?" she queried hopefully one morning when she discovered Sam waiting beside the car for her after breakfast.

"I'm entitled to some holiday time, too, you know," he teased lightly. "Why does it surprise you I should be interested in spending some time with you, seeing the area?"

Jennifer stowed her equipment in the car, partly as an excuse to avoid looking at him.

"Now that Peter has gone away, I expected . . . " Her voice trailed off, and as she straightened, her avoidance tactics failed and her eyes locked with his.

"Peter's a nice kid. As I said, he reminds me of my own brother when he was that age. But he is not the main reason I came here . . . nor the reason I'm staying."

It was on the tip of Jennifer's tongue to ask what the reason was, but she decided against it. She did not think she wanted to know.

She was too confused, too unsure, and Sam's very presence intimidated her. The pain of humiliation that had followed the return of her senses after she had allowed Nigel to turn her head was still acute. She did not want to place herself in that kind of situation again.

Disgruntled at the direction of her thoughts, Jennifer frowned and slid behind the wheel. She was tense as she drove, painfully aware of Sam inches from her. The interior of the car seemed more confined than usual.

They covered the first few miles in silence, and her insides tied themselves in tense knots as she struggled to think of something safe to talk about to ease the atmosphere between them.

"Where are we going today?"

The sound of Sam's voice made her jump. The warm huskiness of it had the unwanted effect of sending a tingle along her nerves.

She took a grip of herself and forced a coolness to her tone she was far from feeling.

"I hoped to spend some time at the Open Air Museum at Singleton."

"So what happens there?" Sam

invited, shifting in his seat to glance at her.

Some of Jennifer's tension ebbed as she spoke, explaining the work carried out by the museum, the traditional buildings they had salvaged and restored, the country crafts and farming methods they practised, the rare breeds, the picturesque setting.

After she had parked the car at the museum, Jennifer led the way through to the site, past the 18th century, timber-framed Hambrook barn.

She adjusted the equipment she was carrying and halted on the grassy slope.

Beside her, Sam whistled in appreciation. She turned to him to suggest he look around for a while, anxious to have some space away from him, and found him watching her, an intense expression in his eyes that she found particularly disturbing.

For a moment she froze, as if mesmerised by that look.

All kinds of unbidden emotions assailed her, frightening her to such an extent that she spun on her heel and walked briskly away from him.

"Jenny, stop."

Her pace slowed with reluctance. Why wouldn't he leave her alone?

He had no business looking at her like that, making her feel things she had no wish to feel. He caught her up and his fingers closed around her wrist.

She looked up to protest, but the words died when she saw the flash of anger he was unable to hide.

"What exactly is it with you?" he demanded.

"Excuse me?"

"This chip you seem to be carrying around on your shoulder." His fingers tightened, denying her attempts to free herself. "Is it just me you have taken a violent dislike to, or all men in general?"

Jennifer knew that her cheeks were on fire.

"I don't know what you're talking about."

"You know exactly what I'm talking about, you just wish you didn't because you don't want to discuss it."

"If you think you know everything, there's not much point in me saying anything," she contended waspishly as she renewed her fruitless struggle to free herself from his grasp.

Her heart thudded against her ribs. If it was obvious to him she did not want him to pry, did not want to talk about it, why did he persist?

Sam tilted his head to one side, a frown on his face.

"You don't want me or anyone else to find you attractive, do you? Why do you want to hide yourself away?"

Confused at his ability to strike at her vulnerable spots, Jennifer lowered her gaze, annoyed with herself for allowing him to harry her.

"I'm just not interested. Not in someone like you."

"What does that mean, someone like me?" he queried with deceptive calm. "You've already made up your mind about me and won't give me a chance. Why not?"

Disturbed by his anger and confused by what he had said, the truth of his words, Jennifer sighed.

"Sam, please, I can't . . . "

His touch became gentle at the thread of despair in her voice, and his own tone was softer.

"Will you tell me his name?"

"Whose?" she asked, playing for time, knowing it was pointless.

"The man who's obviously dented your trust and self-respect."

Jennifer drew in a shaky breath, disturbed by the way in which he unerringly guessed her weaknesses.

As his fingers finally relaxed their hold on her wrist, she withdrew from him and forced herself to meet his gaze.

"Nigel," she finally told him with reluctance.

"What did he do to you?"

She cast an anxious glance in the direction of a family who walked by a short distance away.

"I don't want to talk about this."

"And I don't intend paying for another man's sins."

Jennifer watched in silence as Sam thrust his hands impatiently into the pockets of his jeans and walked away from her, down across the grass towards the main section of the museum. She felt battered from their exchange.

As much as it pained her to admit it, Sam was right. She had taken one look at him and decided there and then how she felt.

But now she had to make re-assessments, Jennifer allowed.

Sam was not the shallow man she had tried to believe, all surface looks and no substance . . . like Nigel.

Jennifer wished Ian was not on holiday. She desperately needed to talk about her anxieties.

He would tease her back to humour, give her advice — and would not be guilty of making judgments as she had done with Sam.

He had supported her during the business with Nigel.

She could hear him now, telling her not to let what Nigel had done stop her from loving anyone else. To do so would mean Nigel had won.

But it was easier said than done. Once bitten, twice shy.

It was hard to trust a second time. And now Ian was not here. She had to face this problem alone and decide what she was going to do.

When Sam eventually rejoined her a couple of hours later, Jennifer had spent almost as much time soul-searching as working.

She looked at him warily as he sat down beside her, but saw none of the annoyance still in his expression.

"I'm sorry," she told him with quiet sincerity.

Her heart gave a curious flip-flop when he turned his head and smiled at her, his eyes warm with understanding and appreciation.

It was as though he knew what the

apology, and the admissions that had brought it about, had cost her, and she could see that as far as he was concerned it was forgotten and they could now move on.

Alarm bells rang at the thought. Jennifer did not know if she wanted to move forward, at least not yet. It was a frightening prospect.

"Friends?"

Sam extended his hand, and Jennifer looked at it for a moment before her gaze lifted to his.

With a brief nod, she tentatively placed her hand in his.

"Friends," she agreed.

Sam smiled at the symbolic gesture and his fingers enfolded hers, warm and firm.

Holding her gaze, he raised her hand to his mouth and kissed her palm. The breath caught in her chest, and she could feel each throb of her pulse as the tingle of awareness at his touch flowed through her.

Disturbed, she withdrew her hand,

thankful that Sam released her and allowed her retreat . . . for now.

"I'm glad you showed me this place," he said with a smile, the atmosphere between them companionable at least. "It's fascinating. I can see why you come back so often. I've just spent ages looking over all the old carpenters' tools."

Jennifer relaxed as they discussed the museum, delighted by Sam's enthusiasm. It made her glad she had shared this with him.

The tension she now felt was more one of nervous anticipation rather than fear, that alarmed and excited at the same time.

After a picnic lunch by the lake, much of which went to feed the ducks, Jennifer lay on her stomach in the shade of a leafy horse chestnut tree and sketched. Sam sat cross-legged beside her making notes for a project he was working on.

She was amazed and a little disconcerted to discover she liked having Sam near her when she worked.

That had never happened with her before, not with her family, her friends, not even with Ian.

Sam's presence did not disturb her . . . at least, not so far as her work was concerned, Jennifer corrected. In all other respects, he was a very disturbing man indeed.

As the afternoon slipped by, Sam went to fetch some ice creams. Jennifer smiled when he returned and handed one to her, and she sat up, biting into the creamy white chocolate with blissful enjoyment.

"Tell me more about your work," Sam encouraged. "Do you have a favourite season to paint?"

"There's something about every time of year that I love. The new growth of spring, the lazy warmth of summer, the rich colours of autumn. But I find the winter incredibly special.

"The trees are so beautiful, the starkness of their skeletons against a winter sky, the way the frost traces every outline of branch and twig . . . the mists . . . that special sunny day when the light is low and clear . . . the iciness . . . the animal tracks in a blanket of snow . . . the silence."

"You should have been a poet, not an artist," Sam said, teasing her.

"I'm one of those lucky people who makes a living from what they love."

"Like me."

Jennifer nodded and found she was empathising with him again. The more she learned about this man, the more time she spent with him, the more she felt she was becoming enmeshed.

He was creeping under her skin and she did not seem to be able to do anything to stop it.

He smiled again and reached across to brush his index finger across the corner of her mouth.

"A bit of chocolate," he explained huskily as he put his finger to his lips and sucked it.

She watched and fought the urge that came, without warning, to kiss him, to experience how those lips would feel against her own.

Her lashes lowered to hide the runaway thought.

But as if obeying some silent command, Sam leaned across and kissed her just the same. Her lips parted in surprise, and before she could come up with any response, he moved away.

"What was that for?" she asked with as much lightness as she could muster.

"Does there have to be a reason?" He smiled. "Take it as a thank you for a lovely day."

★ ★ ★

Jennifer made no objection when Sam accompanied her over the next few days. He was intelligent, fun and sensitive.

He knew just when to back off and give her space. And as the days went by, she enjoyed his company, liked him more than she had expected . . . probably more than was wise.

Towards the end of the week, Jennifer spent some time in her studio, while Sam went to browse in the antique and second-hand bookshops in town.

She had made some good progress with her work, which surprised her given the amount of time she had spent with Sam.

Before lunch, she decided that she needed to go through the photographs she had taken to use for her studio work.

With Ian away, she had left her films to be developed at a local shop, and whilst she begrudged the time a trip to town would take, there were details and colours she needed before she could continue.

Twenty minutes later, she left the shop and walked briskly down the hill, anxious to get back to work, her mind occupied. Suddenly, a voice from nowhere addressed her.

"Well, well, well. If it isn't Jennifer Wilson."

3

JOLTED from her thoughts, Jennifer swung round, unwilling to face the owner of the voice she had come to know so well . . . and to dread. Her eyes clouded when she saw Nigel and a group of his friends.

"Aren't you pleased to see me, Jen?" he mocked with an amused smirk. "Have you been pining for me?"

Determined to ignore him, she turned to walk away, but he grabbed her arm, his fingers biting painfully into her flesh.

"Let me go."

"Why the hurry?" he taunted when she tried to pull her arm away.

His laughter brought angry colour to her cheeks.

"Let me go I said!"

"Aren't you sorry now you didn't take me up on my offer?"

"Not in the least."

Nigel glanced at his friends.

"Still trying to be Miss Goody-goody, pretending to be so innocent and lily-white." He sneered at her, his grip tightening as she struggled to break free. "I could tell some tales of you, Jen."

"Haven't you told enough already?" she snapped at him, hating the way he was laughing at her, showing off in front of his friends. "Does it make you feel good, boost your over-inflated ego?"

His hold on her intensified and she wished she had controlled her temper, not allowed him to bait her. Nigel's blue eyes were cold, his face angry and petulant, and Jennifer wondered what she had ever seen in him.

"Leave me alone," she insisted, but when she attempted to step back, she came up against something solid and a tanned arm encircled her.

"Didn't you hear what she said?" Sam's voice broke in, hard and threatening.

Nigel looked challengingly behind her.

"Keep out of this. It's none of your business."

"Take your hands off her . . . now." His voice was dangerously calm, but Jennifer could feel the tension in Sam's body. "Unless you want to make more of this than necessary?"

Nigel's demeanour changed instantly. Where he had been brash, he now appeared wary, uncertain, and his friends were already walking away calling him to join them.

Jennifer's arm was released and her fingers went to rub the injured spot and restore the circulation. Sam moved her to one side and stepped forward to meet the last of Nigel's resistance. His voice was controlled but his meaning clear.

"If I hear you've bothered Jennifer again, I'll want to know why. Is that understood?"

Nigel stared down at the pavement and mumbled something in the affirmative.

"And there's something else," Sam challenged. "You owe Jennifer an apology."

Nigel's gaze settled on the pavement, unable to meet her eyes.

"I'm sorry."

"Now get out of here," Sam told him. "And don't forget what I said, or you'll answer to me."

As Nigel walked off with his friends, Jennifer glanced around and realised the scene had attracted a large audience. She groaned in despair. Once before Nigel had placed her at the centre of town gossip, and it was not an experience she wished to repeat.

"Are you all right?"

"Yes."

Sam glanced at her and put his arm around her shoulders.

"Keep your chin up and smile," he instructed softly, and she tried to obey as he led her down the hill towards the river.

They walked along the bank for a while until they were out of sight, then she pulled away from him, embarrassed and self-conscious. She watched as the water flowed rapidly upstream with the incoming tide.

"Thank you," she finally murmured, her voice more unsteady than she wished.

"I take it that was Nigel?"

Jennifer nodded in confirmation and looked up into Sam's eyes.

"He hurt you badly?"

Again Jennifer nodded. Sam raised a hand and ran his knuckles lightly down her cheek. She shivered at his touch.

"Did you love him?"

"No." Jennifer turned her head to look back at the river and break the eye contact between them. "I was hurt by what he did, but not by breaking up with him."

She was silent for a while but when she glanced at him, she saw warmth and kindness in the cinnamon depths of his eyes. All of a sudden she wanted to explain. She walked on along the river bank and waited for him to fall into stride with her before she spoke.

"Nigel was new to town. I hadn't known him long when he asked me out six months ago, and I was flattered. I'd had several boyfriends before, nothing too serious — I was more committed to my work.

"I suppose I was attracted to Nigel because he was different, someone unfamiliar, someone I had not been at school with. He was good-looking, charming . . . at least, he was in the beginning."

They crossed a stile and continued along the grassy bank following a bend in the river. Jennifer sat down, drew up her knees and wrapped her arms around them.

"What happened?" Sam prompted as he sat beside her.

Jennifer sighed.

"He kept pushing and pushing, wanting to take the relationship faster and further than I did. Deep down I already had doubts. I know I wasn't ready, and wasn't sure of him or my feelings."

"A good reason to wait." Sam's gaze held hers and the look in his eyes warmed her.

"We had a blazing row when he tried to force the issue. He said if I was holding out for marriage — which had never crossed my mind — I would have a long wait. Besides, he said, it was like buying a car. He'd want a thorough test drive first to see if it was worth the investment."

Sam muttered something under his breath and took her hand, his thumb rubbing circles on her palm.

"Go on."

"He dumped me. But only because I was too slow to do it first," Jennifer added with an attempt at wry humour. "That was when I discovered he had been seeing other people behind my back. What hurt was that everyone had known and let me make an idiot of myself."

"He's the idiot, Jenny, not you."

She shrugged, scrambled to her feet and walked a few steps away.

"The next thing I knew, Nigel was spreading rumours about me. I don't know whether people really believed him or not . . . you know, there's no smoke without fire. I only know that it hurt a lot. I don't understand how anyone can be so spiteful, tell such lies."

"I'm sorry."

Sam moved to stand behind her and slipped his arms around her waist. It was comforting to be held against him and some of her tension ebbed away.

"He won't bother you any more," he reassured her, the words soft against her ear. His lips brushed a gentle kiss across her temple, then he let her go and stepped back. "Now, I suggest we spend the afternoon at the beach and have some fun."

So much for her good intentions at work, Jennifer mused as, back at the house, she changed into a swimsuit and threw some things into her beach bag.

Feeling weak-willed and yet excited at the prospect of this unexpected outing, she went downstairs and joined Sam in the car.

On the short drive to the beach, Jennifer lectured herself she needed to be less transparent. Sam could read her too easily and his understanding and gentle questioning had already led her to divulge more about herself than she intended.

She couldn't help but be wary. Past experience had shaken her confidence and caused her to doubt her judgment where men were concerned. And she really knew very little about Sam, she reminded herself. He was nice, nicer than she had first thought — perhaps too nice?

She cast him a sideways glance then looked back at the road. She had liked Nigel, too — at first. The warning bell rang loud and clear in her head and she would do well to heed it.

Despite the holiday crowds, they found a free space in the carpark and walked along the beach to a less crowded spot. Swiftly removing his shorts and shirt to reveal tanned skin and red trunks, Sam grinned and headed towards the sea at a jog.

"Last one in buys drinks."

Jennifer ignored the challenge and cautioned herself at the awareness she felt when she was with Sam. With a sigh, she took off her sundress and applied some sun cream to her skin before she lay down on her towel.

The sun was hot, and she closed her eyes drowsily, listening to the sounds of laughter as people played on the sand and splashed in the sea. She felt relaxed and content . . . until cold water dripped over her, making her jump and arms scooped her up.

"Put me down at once," she protested.

Sam's hold tightened as she struggled and he strode down the beach.

"Stop fighting!"

"I was enjoying the sun."

"You are not spending the entire afternoon lying on the sand."

Furious that he should tell her what to do, Jennifer renewed her struggles and flung out an arm to hit him when she heard him chuckle. He avoided her, his hand catching hers to prevent a second attempt.

"You're trouble!" He laughed. "You need cooling off."

She screamed as he abruptly released her and she landed in the sea with an undignified splash. As she rose to the surface spluttering with shock and rage, her eyes blazed and her hair was plastered about her face.

That Sam stood in front of her, hands on hips, laughing, only increased her fury.

Jennifer flung herself at him. She caught him by surprise and knocked him off balance, but to her consternation, he caught her and pulled her with him as he fell back into the sea.

"Why, you . . . you . . . " She searched for something sufficiently descriptive.

"Careful, Jenny," he warned teasingly.

"That's not the kind of language you should use in polite company!"

He laughed when he saw the fury in her eyes. With one hand he brushed the wet strands of hair from her face and bent his head to press a firm but gentle kiss to her lips.

"You're lovely when you're angry," he told her softly, relaxing his hold and allowing the movement of the water to separate them. "Come on, I'll race you to that buoy and back."

That kiss, however brief and friendly it had been, had unsettled her, Jennifer admitted as she swam after him. Confusion about her feelings for Sam replaced her earlier anger.

She was on the rebound from one mistake and should pay heed to the anxious voice that continued to issue warnings inside her head if she wanted to avoid the possibility of another.

Casting her concerns aside, she concentrated on Sam's challenge. She was a strong swimmer and used to competition from her brothers, but she had allowed Sam too much distance.

"What kept you?" he teased.

She stopped beside him, dipped her head back under the water to take her hair from her face, then looked at him and smiled.

"You cheated." She laughed at his injured expression. "You had a head start."

"You dawdled."

They stayed in the water for a while, but when Sam took her hand, she allowed him to lead her back up the beach. She towelled herself dry, applied some more sunscreen, then tried to comb her hair into some semblance of order.

Sam had stretched out on his back in the sun, his mirrored glasses shading his eyes from the glare. Jennifer found some change in her bag and went to the kiosk near the carpark to buy drinks.

Sam did not stir when she returned. A mischievous smile curved her mouth and made her eyes sparkle as she leaned over and placed the ice-cold can on his stomach.

With a shocked exclamation, Sam shot up and sent the can rolling to the sand. Jennifer laughed but the smile rapidly left her face when he retrieved the can, shook it and pulled the ring open to send a stream of icy liquid spraying over her.

She jumped to her feet brushing at the stickiness with her towel, unable to help joining in his laughter. Jennifer sat down again and sipped her drink as she watched a group of children playing at the water's edge.

After a while, she glanced at Sam and discovered he was breathing evenly, his hands linked behind his head. She thought he was asleep and allowed her gaze to linger appreciatively on the muscled lines of his tanned body, finding no spare ounce of flesh anywhere.

A slight movement brought her gaze back to his face. As Sam raised his glasses and looked at her, a tinge of colour warmed her cheeks in embarrassment because he had caught her staring at him. She would have turned her face away but for the hand that cupped her chin.

Her tongue unconsciously moistened her lips and Sam's eyes darkened as he followed the movement. His hand slid along her neck to tangle in the drying strands of her hair as he increased the pressure and brought her mouth to his.

Dismayed at her lack of will power, Jennifer did not resist. Indeed, her lips parted in silent invitation. Warning bells rang in her head. This is not sensible, she tried to tell herself. But she ignored her commonsense, and her hand went to rest against his chest to steady her.

Alarmed by the emotions that so quickly assailed her, Jennifer pulled away. Sam let her go, his expression serious as he ran a finger down her cheek.

"Don't be afraid."

"I'm not," she denied, not entirely truthfully, and tore her gaze from his.

"I think you are. Perhaps not just of me but of men in general since Nigel."

He was very astute, Jennifer admitted, but she had already told him too much. When she made no further reply, Sam rose to his feet.

"I'm going to have another swim. I need cooling off this time."

Jennifer watched as he wandered back to the sea, stopping to return a beach ball to some children.

She finished her drink, watching Sam as he swam. She was too unsure of herself to risk any kind of attachment. The bruises Nigel had inflicted had not healed sufficiently.

She could not allow herself to be drawn headlong into another relationship so soon, no matter how attractive she found Sam. And he was attractive, she could not deny it. Not just in a physical sense, but also where it mattered most . . . inside, the real person. He made her laugh, was sensitive to her feelings even when he teased her, was generous, understanding, kind . . .

What was she doing, she chastised herself, writing him a reference? The idea was to reinforce all the reasons she should take care and hold back, not convince herself how wonderful Sam was. She would not — could not — permit herself to rush into anything. Not again.

She was quiet and absorbed in her thoughts when Sam returned from his swim, but aside from casting her a speculative glance, he made no comment. Before long, they decided to leave, and as they reached the carpark, Jennifer heard someone call her name.

She turned to find the Barlow family approaching. They lived down the same lane. She managed to smile, conscious of Sam beside her, and knew she could not avoid introducing him.

"Why did you say I was a 'family friend'?" Sam enquired when they were finally on their way.

"Aren't you?"

"I hope so. But am I not your friend as well?"

"I suppose so." She shrugged and watched from the corner of her eye as he raised an eyebrow. "I'm a member of the family."

Sam smiled then and she felt uncomfortable.

"You're playing with words, Jenny."

"So are you."

4

"THERE you are." Ann Wilson greeted Jennifer and Sam when they arrived home from the beach. "Jen, I completely forgot that your father and I are going to Chichester tonight. I've been in such a rush I haven't done a thing about your supper."

"Don't worry, I'll fix something."

After her mother had gone upstairs, Sam turned to her.

"How about I take you out for dinner tonight?"

"You don't have to do that."

"I know I don't have to. I'd like to." She noticed amusement and a touch of exasperation in his voice. "A simple yes or no would be enough!"

Jennifer bit her lip, uncertain. Which would be safer — to go with him, or stay in the house on their own?

She cleared her throat and forced a lightness to her tone.

"Well, how can I refuse? You're very kind."

Sam laughed, and she realised he had sensed her indecision and knew why she had elected to go with him. She fidgeted under his gaze, warmth in her cheeks.

"Leave the arrangements to me," he told her. "You go and have a bath if you like."

After she had soaked in a deliciously-scented bubble bath, and washed and dried her hair, Jennifer stood wrapped in a towelling robe and surveyed her wardrobe. Her gaze fell on an elegant dress she had purchased on a whim but never had occasion to wear.

It was an exquisite shade of lavender that warmed and enhanced the grey of her eyes. The back was a deep V-cut which dipped below her shoulders, whereas the front neckline was high at the throat, almost demure. The cool, silky fabric was ruched at the hip and the gored skirt gently brushed her knees.

Jennifer applied a light make-up and a dab of her favourite perfume before she gathered her hair and wound it into a neat chignon.

Then she tried on the dress. She stared at her reflection with a nervous jolt. She looked far too . . . A frown creased her brow. She couldn't wear this.

A knock at the door preceded her mother's entrance.

"Your father and I are just leaving . . . Jen!" she exclaimed. "You look stunning. That dress could have been made for you."

Turning back to the mirror, Jennifer chewed her bottom lip. She had not wanted to create that effect.

"Perhaps I should change."

"Whatever for?" Her mother looked horrified. "It's perfect."

With a sigh, Jennifer gathered up her bag and a wrap and allowed her mother to usher her from the room.

They parted in the hall and Jennifer walked to the living-room, suddenly shy. She was able to observe Sam for a few moments before he became aware of her presence.

She had never seen him formally dressed before. His lightweight, mid-grey suit hung perfectly from his lean frame, and his crisp, white shirt was offset with a red and grey tie. He looked incredibly handsome.

At that moment he turned and the glass in his hand halted in mid-air as his gaze fixed on her. His expression held appreciation, a hint of surprise and something else she did not wish to define. It caused goose-bumps to form on her arms. Jennifer swallowed and continued into the room.

"Can I pour you a drink?"

Jennifer shook her head. Her hands were shaking too much.

Sam placed his glass on the sideboard and closed the distance between them. He took one of her hands in his and raised it to his lips to press a kiss to the inside of her wrist.

"You look lovely."

"Thank you."

He lifted his free hand and trailed his fingers along her cheek. The touch was so light she could almost have imagined it but for the tingling sensation she experienced.

He was so close now, the faint scent of his musky aftershave reaching her, increasing her awareness of him. Warily, Jennifer took a step back. He smiled, a special smile that melted her insides.

"Come on," he said softly, breaking the spell and releasing her. "It's time to go."

Jennifer pulled herself together and, on the way to the car, told herself several times to calm down and not allow things to get out of hand. Sam smiled across at her as he fastened his seatbelt, then started the engine of his car and drove down the lane.

By the time they had covered a few miles, Jennifer realised where they were headed. She looked across at Sam, her grey eyes wide.

"Are we going to the Old Priest House?"

"Anything wrong with that?"

"N — no," Jennifer stammered. "It's just that it's very . . . "

She came to a sudden stop. Intimate was the word that sprang to her mind.

"Your mother recommended it. She said it was very . . . nice."

His pause was intentional, she was sure, and she threw him a startled glance. Could he really read her mind? Or maybe it was just that she was easy to see through. She looked away as the restaurant came into view.

The building was old, built of sandstone, the upper storey whitewashed and of post and panel construction. The roof was thatched and sported a squat brick chimney.

Jennifer knew of its reputation but had never been herself — none of her previous boyfriends had been out-to-dinner kind of dates. Not to somewhere like this, anyway.

She tensed when she realised what she had thought. Previous boyfriends, as if she were now unconsciously classing Sam in the boyfriend category. Jennifer gave herself a mental shake as they left the car and went inside.

The restaurant itself was divided, secluded, allowing privacy, and the realisation did nothing to calm her nerves. The table for two to which they were shown heightened her tension. As if he sensed her discomfort, Sam kept the conversation light to allow her time to relax.

"I presume this house once belonged to the parish church?" he asked once they had given their orders.

"Yes, it was built by the priory. It's dated in the early thirteenth century, I think, although the upper floor is later."

When their starters arrived, Jennifer found herself relaxing. Sam was excellent company, funny, sensitive, attentive . . . if only she was not so wary, so afraid to allow herself to care for anyone again.

They lingered over the meal. Jennifer had chosen the chicken rolled with crab and onion, Sam the Dover sole. The food was delicious, perfectly cooked and attractively served, and the light and fruity wine Sam had ordered blended well.

"I couldn't manage another thing," Jennifer protested when Sam suggested she have a dessert to finish off her meal. Although she had noticed they looked delicious when she saw them presented in the chilled cabinet.

"How about coffee?" Sam smiled.

"Definitely a better idea."

It was well after nine when Sam called for the bill. She could not believe how quickly the time had slipped by, and now she was reluctant for the evening to end. On the way home she was unable to stop thinking about him.

"You haven't been out with your friends much since I've known you," he startled her by commenting. "Why is that?"

"I don't know." Jennifer was grateful for the dimness in the car. "When I was seeing Nigel I just seemed to lose touch with my old crowd . . . "

Sam threw her a thoughtful glance. "And with the way things ended you're anxious about being accepted again?" he asked softly.

"Maybe. I hadn't really thought about it," she replied, wishing he were not so perceptive.

"What are we going to do with you, Jenny?"

"I don't know what you mean."

"Yes, you do," he countered as he turned off the main road and into the lane. "I understand how you feel but you can't keep shutting out the world. People like you because you're you — if they know you, it won't matter to them what an idiot like Nigel says. Not unless you make it matter."

Jennifer remained silent. She knew he was right but she did not want to discuss it, especially with him. He was too clever at probing inside her head, analysing her feelings. Nigel's actions had hurt her, and her trust and confidence could not be rebuilt overnight.

When Sam stopped the car in front of the house, Jennifer scrambled out and opened the front door before he could move too close. She switched on the lights in the hall and the living-room then hovered inside, watching Sam warily. Her nervousness had returned.

"Would you like something to drink?"

"Another coffee would be nice," he replied.

Jennifer took her time in the kitchen. Her insides had tied themselves in knots and she was so aware of him it frightened her. She had to get a grip on herself, she admonished, as she poured out the coffee.

Unable to prolong her return any longer, she carried the cups through to the living-room. In her absence, Sam had discarded his jacket, loosened his tie, and selected a soft, classical CD from her father's collection. He had also turned down the dimmer switch on the lights. Her sense of uncertainty increased.

He sat on the settee, his long legs stretched out in front of him. His hair was ruffled, as if he had recently run his fingers through it, one of the characteristic gestures she was coming to recognise.

He accepted his coffee with a word of thanks and smiled when she chose to sit in an armchair some feet away from him.

"So?" he asked after a moment.

"So what?" Jennifer looked up from her cup to see Sam staring intently at her with his searching eyes.

"Are you going to hide away for ever, Jenny?"

"I'm not hiding away," she refuted, a little too hotly. She was annoyed at his continued insistence. Why must he spoil what had been an enjoyable evening? "Stop bullying me."

284

"Is that what you think I'm doing?"

She shrugged in response.

"That's what it seems like sometimes."

Sam set his cup on the table and stood up, holding out a hand to her.

"Come here." When she refused, he walked across and drew her gently to her feet.

"Dance with me."

He held Jennifer close and she rested her hands against his chest, feeling the warmth of his skin through the fabric of his shirt. Her mouth felt dry, and her own skin tingled from the touch of his fingers as they moved lightly over her back.

The music was slow and soft. Sam pulled her closer and his hands moved to her hair, pulling out the pins to allow it to fall and frame her face. One hand remained at the nape of her neck and rubbed soothingly back and forth. His other hand cupped her chin and tilted her face to his.

Jennifer gazed into the warm, cinnamon eyes, then felt the touch of his lips as he kissed her eyes closed. He teased her, brushing kisses at the corners of her mouth, pulling back when she would try to deepen the contact.

Realising his lips were no longer on hers, Jennifer's eyes fluttered open. He was watching her, his face serious, his own eyes dark with desire.

She tentatively touched his face, her good intentions flying out of the window. One kiss wouldn't hurt, she attempted to convince herself. Just one . . .

The shrill intrusion of the telephone brought a groan from Sam, and Jennifer began to wonder if it were providential, saving her from a moment of madness.

She cleared her throat and tore her gaze from the burning expression on Sam's face before she answered it.

"Hello? Peter! How are you getting on?" Out of the corner of her eye, she saw Sam move across to the stereo system. "You've broken your arm? How did you manage that?"

"I fell off a wall," her brother told her. "They're sending me home tomorrow. I tried to persuade John to stay, but he's coming with me. The train gets in at four o'clock. Can you pick us up?"

"Of course. Is it painful?" she asked, hearing an unusual strain in her brother's voice.

"A bit. It's not too bad. Is Sam still there?"

Jennifer glanced across the room.

"Yes, he is. Do you want to talk to him?"

She ignored Sam's frown and negative shake of his head. Her common sense had returned, and however cowardly, she was not about to pass up this opportunity to call a halt to the evening.

"Yes, please, Jen," Peter confirmed.

"I'll say goodbye and hand you over. I'll tell Mum and Dad in the morning. Take care, Peter."

Jennifer put her hand over the

mouthpiece and held the receiver out to Sam. To say he was displeased with her would be an understatement, she acknowledged, and the annoyance in his eyes almost quelled her. As he took the phone, she slipped from his grasp and moved to the door.

"Thank you for a lovely evening, Sam. I really enjoyed it."

She heard him mutter something at her retreating back as she scurried up the stairs to the safety of her bedroom.

Once there, she sat on her bed, lost in thought. After Sam's comments on her current lack of social life and his attempts to encourage her to make a new start after Nigel, had the whole evening been some kind of experiment? Perhaps the dim lights and smoochy music had been a ploy and had meant nothing to him at all?

Jennifer sighed. She did not want to think that, but how could she be sure? Nothing in life and love was sure, an inner voice pointed out. One had to take a chance. But was she ready? Could she trust again . . . not only in a man, but also in herself to make the right decision?

After a troubled night, Jennifer woke at dawn to another glorious summer day. She had a quick shower, then dressed in a loose-fitting, multi-coloured cotton dress that tied over each shoulder in a bow, and slipped her feet into a pair of lace-up pumps.

In the kitchen, she met her father preparing early-morning tea, and relayed the message about Peter. She made herself some toast and poured a glass of milk from the fridge, enjoying her hasty breakfast before she collected her sketch book, camera and threw together a packed lunch. She needed some space and time to herself to think.

She let herself out of the house and went round to the garage to collect her bicycle. There was a trace of heaviness in the air. Only the gentlest of breezes stirred the uppermost branches of the trees that screened the house and apart from the excited chatter of the wrens who were nesting in a hedge nearby, there was nothing to disturb the peace of the morning.

Jennifer halted by the side of the house to admire her mother's vast array of sweet peas, relishing the glorious scent. Pink and blue clematis entwined with old-fashioned roses and climbed the lower walls of the whitewashed house.

She moved on and unlocked the door of the garage. She located her bike, relieved to find the tyres hard and in good condition.

There was a large wicker basket on the front, into which she put her camera, materials and her picnic. Just as she was about to extricate her bike, an amused voice sounded behind her and had her spinning round.

"Running away?"

5

SAM lounged indolently in the doorway, his arms folded across his chest. He made her feel like a small child caught getting up to some mischief, Jennifer thought crossly, as a wave of colour suffused her face.

"I have work to do." She was on the defensive and it didn't suit her. Wheeling the bike towards the door, she tried to pass him. "Excuse me."

Sam made no attempt to stand aside. "I'll come with you if you like."

Jennifer's hackles rose. Did he have to sound as if he were doing her a big favour by granting her his company?

"I don't like."

"Scared?"

The taunt was delivered half-amused, half-challenging, but the expression in his eyes gave nothing away.

"Suit yourself," she snapped ungraciously, and pushed past him into the open air.

He turned to watch her and his gaze travelled slowly over her from her head to her toes and back again in a most provocative and disturbing manner.

Jennifer's blood started to boil — and not just with temper she acknowledged, a fact which made her crosser than ever.

"What's the matter?" she demanded, her irritation getting the better of her.

"Nothing's the matter with me."

"Meaning what, exactly?"

Sam sent her a lazy smile.

"Meaning nothing, exactly . . . meaning whatever you like." He paused for a moment, but when she refused to spar with him, he raised an eyebrow. "Is there a bike I can borrow?"

"In there," she told him, nodding towards the garage's dark interior. "Help yourself — you will anyway." When he continued to stand there staring at her, she almost stamped her foot with frustration. "Well, hurry up if you're coming. I don't intend to waste the entire day!"

"My, my, we are touchy today!"

Sam disappeared inside the garage while Jennifer seethed with rage outside. He was the most infuriating man she'd ever met. The last thing she wanted was to be forced to spend the rest of the day with him.

When at last he rejoined her outside, she slammed the door, locked it and pocketed the key before pedalling down the drive and off up the lane at a furious pace. Sam's laughter behind her inflamed her temper.

With effortless ease, he caught her up and adjusted his pace to hers. The day would be hot and sticky, and she already regretted her impetuous start, without the added problem of her skirt.

The breeze created by the speed of the bike made the fabric dance and flutter and show an over-generous amount of leg. She tried in vain to restore some decorum, and the fact that Sam was laughing openly at her made her furious.

"Having problems?"

She threw him a furious glare, her temper well and truly stoked. If only she had worn shorts, like him, she rued, but then she had not anticipated company, had she? Of course, he looked cool and untroubled. He was never any different!

"Don't you have some work to do, articles to write?" she snapped, half in anger, half in hope.

"Nothing that can't wait," he assured her with another of those irritating, lazy smiles. "Really, Jenny, you must be careful or I'll think you don't want my company!"

Jennifer had never hit anyone in her life but she had a burning desire to do so now. Just the thought of wiping that mocking grin from his face brought a flash of satisfaction.

Their pace slowed, and Jennifer admitted she had allowed her temper to better her. After a while, she pulled off the road and cycled down a track that led to the river, through a gate, which she carefully shut behind them, and on to the footpath that ran along the bank.

They pushed their bikes and savoured the views in all directions. After crossing a footbridge over the river, they cycled through a hamlet and down a country lane.

Despite her preoccupation and her previous mood, Jennifer found herself relaxing. The hedgerows were alive with colour, the scents of the wild flowers, the multitude of butterflies and bees and small birds. In the fields on either side of the road, they saw rabbits and partridges. A kestrel hovered over the headland a short distance away.

That Sam appreciated what he saw pleased Jennifer. She found her local area so beautiful and fascinating, and she loved to find that enthusiasm in others. Contrarily, she was glad now that she had shared this with him.

They free-wheeled down the high-banked hill to the hamlet of South Stoke, with its attractive church, fine houses and its secluded serenity on the bank of the Arun.

It was a unique and peaceful setting, and a place Jennifer loved to visit and sketch. She propped her bike against the footbridge and suggested Sam look at the church while she worked.

Jennifer gathered her equipment, climbed the stile and went to sit on the riverbank. For a moment, she merely observed her surroundings, breathed the sweet air and savoured the country smells she knew so well.

Then she started to work and for the next two hours nothing could have broken her concentration. She had many canvasses to complete before her show.

She was aware of Sam before he reached her later that morning, but apart from a nod of acknowledgement, Jennifer carried on with her work, determined to make some headway.

Sam stretched out on the bank by her side, removed his shirt and soaked up the sun.

Most of the morning slipped away, and Jennifer was frustrated that she had not accomplished more. Her mind refused to concentrate. She packed away her pencils, closed her pad and drew her knees up as she enjoyed the view.

"I loved the church." Sam sat up beside her and smiled.

"I'm glad."

She glanced at him and diverted her gaze from his bare chest, clasping her hands around her knees to prevent them succumbing to the urge to reach out and touch him. What had he done to her, this man she barely knew?

There was so much about him and his life yet to discover, so many questions unanswered. How could she feel such a pull towards him after such a short time?

"Jenny?"

"Mmm?"

Unable to help herself, she turned to look at him. The serious expression she found there surprised her. It was an expression that sparked fresh worries inside her and she jumped to her feet to try and break the spell of the moment.

He watched as she picked up her belongings.

"Where are you going?"

"I've finished here. I want to move on, and I must get home early to go and meet Peter." Jennifer could hear herself babbling.

In one lithe movement, Sam was on his feet, and he reached for her before she could avoid him. He buried his hand in her hair and exerted enough pressure to make her look at him. Whether he read some of the panic she was feeling, she did not know, but with a shake of his head, he sighed and released her.

She could feel the effects of his touch long after he had withdrawn it, and it maddened her that such an innocuous contact should arouse such a welter of emotions inside her.

Sam thrust his hands into the pockets of his shorts, an uncharacteristically brooding expression on his face. For a long moment he studied her, then turned away. He pulled on his shirt, drew his mirrored glasses from his pocket and set off along the path leaving her to follow in his wake.

Jennifer acknowledged, as she trailed after him, that a change had taken place in their relationship over the last couple of days. The awareness was the same as ever, but it was heightened now by a new tension that threatened to boil over and swamp her.

Back on their bikes, they continued along the riverbank. After a while, they stopped for lunch, and Jennifer shared hers with Sam. She wasn't hungry. It had become unbearably hot, the atmosphere close and heavy.

Sam frowned at her.

"Are you all right?"

"Apart from the heat."

"It's turned very humid and muggy," he agreed. "Why aren't you eating?"

"I'm not very hungry." Jennifer shrugged. "Probably the weather," she excused lamely, and she could tell by Sam's expression he was unconvinced. Glancing round, she noticed that a murderous-looking black cloud was bearing down on them from the far side of the hill. "Look."

"It's going to pour before long." He began to pack their things back on the bikes. "Is there somewhere we can shelter?"

"There's an old barn in a field on the other side of that wood. We may make it in time."

Jennifer led the way, guiding them back to the lane where they would make faster progress. She cut across a wooded track and was halfway through when the first rumble of thunder rocked the sky. The air was horribly thick.

The storm broke with a frightening flash of lightning and another deafening crash of thunder. They were in sight of

300

the barn when the rain began to fall in torrents, the drops so large they stung her flesh.

Soaked to the skin, Jennifer grabbed her sketchbook and camera, dropped her bike and scrambled over the metal hurdles that barricaded the entrance to the barn. Sam vaulted over beside her and drew her inside the dry shelter.

She set her things down on a hay bale in a stack in one corner and quickly examined her camera for water damage. It looked all right, but she would have Ian check it.

Another blinding flash and ear-splitting crash made her jump, and she laughed at herself as she huddled into the hay.

Outside, the rain continued to fall. The sky was black, the countryside turned to a murky, bleak landscape, but Jennifer knew these summer storms often stopped as quickly as they started. At least it should clear the heavy atmosphere.

Sam moved to sit in the hay near

her and she felt the spark of awareness that had become so familiar . . . too familiar. In an effort to keep some distance between them, emotional as much as physical, she rose and walked across to lean against the side of the barn and watched the rain.

When she turned, it was to discover Sam was staring intently at her. She cleared her throat and injected a lightness she did not feel to her voice.

"Why did you choose sports journalism?" Jennifer asked, interested to learn more about him and to keep the conversation away from herself.

"I'm a sports addict." Sam smiled, leaning back against the bales, relaxed. "Being a jack of some sports and a master of none, I certainly didn't have the talent to be a professional footballer, or golfer. The next best thing was to write about it."

Jennifer gave him an apologetic shrug.

"I know nothing about sport."

"And I can't even draw pin-men to scale!"

Jennifer returned his grin.

"You must have been to some interesting places."

He nodded in confirmation.

"Some wonderful, some not so good. Comes with the territory. But I've made a lot of friends, met many of my sporting heroes . . . I enjoy it."

One of the things Jennifer liked about Sam was his modesty. She remembered his conversation with her father, how he had played down the fact that he had won the Sports Journalist of the Year Award three times running, how the books he had written had become bestsellers.

Now, to her, he talked about it with simplicity and evident pleasure, with not a touch of ego.

"Where do you go next?" she asked, keeping her tone neutral. These few days off were bound to end soon and she was disturbed by her growing reluctance for him to leave. If he had detected any hint of her feelings she was grateful he ignored it.

"I'm working on a biography," he told her, naming an international footballer who had died in a tragic accident at the height of his career.

"Even I've heard of him."

Sam nodded, a frown creasing his brow.

"It's turning out to be something of a tragic story altogether. He had a bad childhood, became a world-class footballer despite the odds, then was struck down just as the success he had dreamed of, all his ambitions were within reach."

"That's sad." Jennifer's gaze locked with his for a moment and, unsettled, she looked away. "What then?"

"Usual coverage of the football season, and I've been offered the chance to do some radio work as well. I've never done that before."

Jennifer smiled and thought he would be good at that. He had the kind of voice that was easy to listen to. Warm, slightly husky, and with his enthusiasm for the subject and his knowledge, it would open up new avenues for him.

"Enough about me," he asserted just as further questions formed in her mind. "Come and sit down."

Reluctantly, Jennifer did so, nervous when he took her hand and pulled her down beside him, closer than was necessary. She stared anxiously out at the rain.

"I wonder how long it will last."

"Why the hurry?"

"I just have things to do," she prevaricated and tried without success to withdraw her hand. "Sam . . . "

"Look at me."

Against her will, she did as he said, and she attempted to swallow the lump that lodged in her throat. She knew he was going to kiss her. Part of her ached for him to, but it had already happened once too often for Jennifer's liking.

He watched the play of emotions across her face then slowly leaned forward to press a featherlight kiss to her lips.

When he pulled back a fraction, she dreaded what he would see in her eyes. His fingers threaded into her damp hair and he drew her mouth to his.

Although her mind told her she must resist, insisted she could pull away now, before it was too late, her body would not obey. Instead she remained captured, a moth to the flame.

He eased her back until they were lying in the hay. To her mortification, her lips parted in invitation and she returned his burning kiss. Her fingers sank into his thick, unruly hair as they had ached so long to do.

"Jenny . . . "

He breathed her name against her skin as he trailed his lips down her throat. She bit her lip and tried not to become too involved.

Outside the barn, the storm was dying, but now, it seemed, there was a fresh storm raging with growing intensity inside herself. Her heart pounded wildly against her ribs.

"No!"

She pushed against him, panicked by the way she lost control the instant he touched her.

"Jenny — "

"Don't . . . please."

Sam released her and she scrambled to her feet, trying to think. He watched her. She could feel his gaze burning into her.

"I'm sorry," she murmured. "I can't. This isn't what I want."

"What do you want?"

She turned to face him, surprised at the chill in his eyes.

It was only what she deserved, she told herself. She had not been fair. Sam could not be blamed for her contrariness. In fact, he had been patient with her.

"Well?" he prompted.

"I just want us to be friends."

He raised a mocking brow.

"Friends?"

"Yes." She twisted her fingers together

nervously. "This is happening too fast, Sam. I need time. And I really know nothing about you, do I?"

Sam snatched his damp shirt from the hay and pulled it on.

"What more do you need to know before you will admit there is something between us?"

"How do I know? You'll be going away soon, and you may be in a relationship already. You may even be married for all I know."

"I see." She flinched at the angry expression in his narrowed eyes. "What do you think?"

"I don't know."

"Then let me know when you find out."

"Sam, please . . ."

"Please what? Please stop, please go? What is it you want of me?"

"I want you to understand. I want us to go back to — "

"Being friends?" he interrupted with an ironic smile.

Jennifer nodded.

For several moments he did not speak. He seemed to be fighting some inner battle as he stared at her, his eyes hard. A muscle pulsed in his jaw. When he spoke, his voice was flat and expressionless.

"If that's what you want, then that's how it'll be." He glanced outside. "The rain's stopped. Get your things, it's time to go."

6

JENNIFER threw her energies into the preparation of her exhibition with dogged determination.

In the week since Sam had left, she had been disconcerted by how much she missed him. She thought about him constantly and often found herself sketching him without conscious thought.

The tense atmosphere between them since the incident in the barn had not dissipated. Even Peter's arrival home and his detailed report of his holiday and his accident had failed to lighten the mood.

Her brother had been disappointed by Sam's decision to leave, her parents surprised.

Sam had handled them with suave charm, but Jennifer had known the reason for his rapid departure. She felt guilty and disappointed.

He had promised to return, but would he? Was it just politeness, or genuine intent? Jennifer was uncertain.

Nor was she sure of her feelings, if she wanted him to return, or was glad they had made the clean break.

She did not feel glad. It was as if, in the short time she had known him, he had filled a gap. Now he was gone, she felt empty.

Jennifer snapped out of her reverie when her mother came into the studio.

"I've brought you a sandwich and some coffee, love."

"Oh, Mum, that's sweet, but you shouldn't have troubled."

"You've been working so hard," her mother complained. "And skipping meals. You're very pale."

"I'm fine." Jennifer smiled. "You know what I'm like at exhibition time," she prevaricated, using the excuse her mother had offered to explain her recent loss of appetite.

"Mmm. You seem well ahead this

year," her mother agreed as she looked over some of the paintings Jennifer had laid out before she moved to the table. "These sketches of Sam are excellent. I didn't know you were working on these."

Jennifer looked startled. She had forgotten she had left them there and wished her mother had not found them. A tinge of colour washed her face and she felt as though she'd been caught out.

"I — "

"I get the feeling that you quite like him, Jen."

"He's . . . all right, I suppose," she murmured non-committally unable to meet her mother's gaze.

"He fitted in so well, almost like one of the family. Your father and I like him immensely, so does Peter, of course. You spent some time with him, I rather hoped — "

"Mum," she interrupted warningly, her eyebrows knitting together in a frown.

"Not all men are like Nigel."

"I know that."

"Well . . . "

Jennifer saw hope mixed with understanding on her mother's gentle face.

"Now stop. I can see what you're thinking. Sam and I are friends. That's all. We enjoy each other's company."

"If you say so, dear." Ann Wilson sighed. "But . . . " She hesitated but Jennifer refused to be drawn. "Well, I'll leave you to get on then."

"Mum," Jennifer called as her mother reached the door. "Thanks for the sandwich. I hadn't realised how hungry I was."

Before Jennifer knew it, the exhibition was upon her. Consumed with nerves, as she was each year, she spent ages hanging her paintings . . . then moving most of them again.

She was a prolific artist, and this annual show was always well attended with plenty of buyers and a healthy percentage of new contacts. Even so,

Jennifer never took her success for granted.

Sometimes, she half expected the bubble to burst and had nightmares that no-one would come, or that none of her work would sell.

By the end of the week, Jennifer felt completely drained. The days had passed in a frantic rush and she could not believe how busy the exhibition had been.

Her feet ached, and her throat was sore from hours of endless conversation and answering questions. She was so tired, she was looking forward to the final hour and the moment she was able to close the door behind the last of the stragglers.

"Hi."

Jennifer swung round at the sound of Sam's voice. Her breath caught in her throat at the sight of him . . . tall, and heart-stoppingly handsome. With a struggle she regained her composure and smiled.

"This is a surprise."

314

His eyes twinkled as he gave her a conspiratorial wink.

"Don't tell anyone, but I'm playing hookey."

"Ah!" Jennifer dropped her voice to a hushed whisper. "Your secret's safe with me."

"Can I have a look round?"

"Help yourself."

She allowed him to wander on his own and tried to concentrate on sorting through her list of sales to be ready for those customers who would collect their purchases when the exhibition ended that afternoon. But she could not stop glancing at him out of the corner of her eye.

What did he think of her work? His opinion mattered, she acknowledged and felt a nervous flutter in her stomach. By the time Sam came back to perch on the edge of her table, she was on tenterhooks.

"Your paintings are fantastic."

A flush of pleasure coloured her skin. Sam's sincere praise meant more to

Jennifer than all the effusive compliments she had received during the rest of the week.

"Thank you."

"You're welcome."

For a moment their eyes met. Jennifer swallowed and looked away to break the contact that had affected her like a physical touch.

Sam straightened and stepped away.

"I can see it has been a success by the number of red dots on the frames."

"I know. I can't believe it."

"I bet you say that every year." He smiled and she gave a wry shrug. "Never doubt your talent, Jenny. It's special."

"Thank you . . . again."

She was still glowing from his compliment when the first of the buyers arrived, and by the time it was over, only the final clearing remained.

She packed the uncollected pictures into her car, and with Sam's help, finished the last of the packing and tidying.

★ ★ ★

"I think I could sleep for a week," Jennifer complained at supper that night.

It was a light-hearted meal. Jennifer was flushed with success, Peter was over the moon that Sam was back and bombarded him with questions, commandeering his attention, while her parents were happy and content, watching the family scene unfolding before them.

Afterwards, they sat in the living-room. Sam paid her scant attention, and Jennifer found she was irrationally piqued by his new attitude. She watched him from beneath her lashes.

This arrangement had been her idea, she admitted grumpily, and yet she was inordinately disappointed.

It was ridiculous, she chastised herself. While she was more aware of him than ever, he appeared to have no trouble at all in treating her as a friend.

His apparent lack of awareness of her had taken the gloss off her elation. She pretended that it was down to being tired. She had got precisely what she wanted and nipped Sam's advances in the bud. She should be happy about it. But she wasn't. And that fact both annoyed and frightened her.

The ring of the doorbell jerked her from her thoughts. Her father went to answer it, and after a few intriguing noises from the hall and muffled laughter, he returned with a broad smile on his face.

He stepped aside and a tall, slim-built young man with over-long dark hair, startling blue eyes and boyish dimples walked into the room.

"Ian!"

Jennifer leaped from her chair and dashed across the room. He wrapped his arms around her and hugged her tight.

318

"Hello, gorgeous."

"It's wonderful to see you," Ann Wilson greeted when the furore of his arrival had died down. "When did you get back?"

"About ten minutes ago! I've not even been home yet and my bags are blocking your hall." He grinned. "Have I missed your cooking!"

"If you're angling for a dinner invitation, we've already eaten," Jennifer's mother teased.

Ian gave her a cheeky wink.

"Shame. Still, there's always tomorrow!"

"Sit down, and I'll make you a sandwich."

As her mother left, Jennifer extracted herself from Ian's embrace and returned to her chair, conscious of Sam's watchful gaze. Her father put his arm around Ian's shoulder.

"You won't have met Sam."

"No," Ian replied, shaking hands. He shot an enquiring glance at Jennifer. "Nice to meet you, Sam."

"You, too."

Alarmed by the cool politeness in Sam's voice, Jennifer shot a look at him, and met an intense, unreadable expression in his eyes. Maybe she hadn't explained to him about Ian? She had not been able to interpret that grim expression, but he looked decidedly annoyed with her.

When her mother arrived back with a doorstop sandwich, Ian slid on to the arm of Jennifer's chair and balanced the plate on one jean-clad thigh.

"Sorry I missed the exhibition," he apologised between mouthfuls. "Traffic Controllers' strike. You can give me a private viewing later! I can't wait to see your work for this year."

Jennifer grinned, but her smile dimmed as she intercepted Sam's glower. His eyes narrowed as she boldly returned his stare and refused to be intimidated by his sudden ill-humour.

As Peter told Ian of his accident and launched into detail of his meeting with Sam, Jennifer managed to look away.

"Jennifer said you were in The

Gambia?" Sam asked at length.

"It was fantastic." Ian nodded. "I've got some great shots. I can't wait to develop my films."

He chatted for a while about his trip then turned to Jennifer.

"Fancy a drink?"

She glanced at Sam, but his eyes were blank of expression.

"Why not? I'll be with you in a moment."

That was so typical of Sam, she thought as she ran upstairs to fetch her bag. Why glare at her one moment and be icily withdrawn the next?

Jennifer enjoyed her evening at the pub. They met up with some of the old crowd, and she was touched by their obvious pleasure at seeing her. Sam had been right. She had worried for nothing.

"Tell me about Sam," Ian instructed as they walked home arm in arm.

"What about him?" she hedged.

"Whatever there is to tell!"

"Nothing."

"You expect me to believe that?" Ian chuckled. "The air positively sizzled between you."

"Nonsense." Jennifer dismissed him with a snap. "You're imagining things. He's simply a family friend."

"Keep saying it, Jen, and you may even convince yourself."

Jennifer snapped on the hall light when they reached the house.

"Do you want a coffee?" she asked, stepping round his cluster of abandoned luggage.

"I knew it," Ian joked triumphantly, wrapping his arms around her. "You've been trying to get me on my own all evening. Are you going to invite me up to that intimate, little studio of yours to examine your etchings, as well?"

Jennifer laughed, then sobered as Ian released her, his eyebrows rising in amusement as he glanced behind her.

She turned to see Sam framed in the living-room doorway. Surely he hadn't been waiting up? And had he been listening to their meaningless banter?

Ian winked at her and picked up his bags.

"I won't have coffee now, Jen! I'll catch up with you tomorrow."

He placed a firm kiss on her startled mouth and walked down the drive. Jennifer closed the door with slow deliberation, a curious knot in the pit of her stomach.

She could feel Sam's gaze boring into her back, took a deep breath and turned to face him with a forced smile.

"Were you just going up?" she asked lightly.

He nodded, his eyes narrowed and intense.

"It's late. I thought you would have been home a while ago."

"I was having a pleasant evening."

"You said you were tired," he reminded her.

"I needed to unwind after the strain of the week. How better than with friends?" She cocked an eyebrow at him. "I thought you were encouraging me to go out more?"

He stared at her for a long moment, and she watched the rapid rise and fall of his Adam's apple in the tanned column of his throat as he swallowed. His jaw tightened and he lowered his gaze.

"So I was. Good-night, Jenny."

She watched in silence as he turned and went up the stairs to the spare room. She felt deflated. This uneasy relationship with Sam was not working out as she had intended. With a deep sigh, she checked the locks and went up to bed.

Unable to sleep, she tossed and turned for ages, staring at the shadows on her ceiling. Finally, she threw back the light duvet, pulled on a wrap and tiptoed up to her studio.

Normally after exhibition week, she slept like a log. Now she felt too tense, filled with restless energy and a growing sense of inner dissatisfaction.

Sam had slipped calmly into the rôle she had created for him and it made her wonder if any feeling he had had for her had been genuine. Perhaps she had been no more than a diversion, an amusement, after all?

Absently, Jennifer opened her sketch-book and looked at the drawings she had made of Sam. An idea for a portrait composition formed in her mind. It was an urge she could not deny. Carried away by a burst of enthusiasm, she made some notes and preliminary drafts.

Two hours later, she yawned and looked at her ideas shaping up on paper with satisfaction. She would make a proper start on the picture tomorrow, she decided. Stifling another yawn, she went back to bed.

Jennifer overslept, and by the time she went downstairs the next morning, Sam had left. She swallowed a wave of disappointment as her mother imparted the news, anger at her reaction gnawing at her.

He was a busy man. And there was nothing to keep him here, she added to herself as she prepared a cup of coffee and a piece of toast and carried them up to her studio.

Over the next week, she threw herself into her work, but set aside some time each day to devote to Sam's portrait. She had decided to do a composite . . . a series of pictures in different poses on the same canvas, linked together and yet separate. It was taking shape better than she had hoped.

A plan began to form in her mind. She knew that Sam's birthday was in a few weeks, and if she had the portrait ready, she would give it to him. Maybe, by then, she would feel less confused about her own feelings and would be able to view her awareness of him more clearly.

She just knew that she could not go on like this indefinitely. Sam had only been gone for a few hours and already the hollow ache inside her had begun to make her feel very empty indeed.

7

THE night was still warm, the sky clear and seemed to stretch away for ever into the velvet blackness.

The barbecue had begun an hour or more ago and was now in full swing. A bonfire glowed, sending out a fierce heat, crackling and hissing on the sand. Someone in the crowd had brought a cassette player and couples were dancing to the taped music, shapely silhouettes against the flames.

Once a year Jennifer's circle of friends held this beach party to mark the start of the Festival in the village and it was open to all. Jennifer sat in front of Ian and leaned back against his legs, biting into the hamburger he had just fetched for her.

Dressed in jeans rolled up to the knees, her feet were bare and her toes curled in the sand. The night air was warm enough not to have to worry about a jacket.

Ian's fingers played with her ponytail and he tweaked it teasingly as he reminded her of childhood memories.

She was laughing at him when her gaze drifted towards the table that held the drinks, beside which two bikini-clad girls were handing out the food.

A figure caught her eye. Jennifer stiffened as Sam, with Peter behind him, began to move in their direction.

Ian sensed her change of mood, glanced down and then followed the direction of her gaze.

"Interesting," he murmured in her ear as he placed a hand either side of her neck and leaned forward.

"What is?"

"A sudden rise in temperature and a rapid thumping of the heart," Ian diagnosed as his fingers slipped round and found the wildly beating pulse at her throat. "What should the medical world deduce from that?"

Angry colour rushed to Jennifer's face and she shrugged his hands away and clambered to her feet. She glared at him.

"There is nothing to deduce from anything. I'm hot, that's all."

"This is me, Ian, your constant friend and companion since we were in nappies. Don't try and pull the wool over my eyes. I know you better than anyone. I'd say you have the hots all right, but not in the way you mean."

Having started in a teasing fashion, Ian had suddenly become serious. Jennifer stared at him with horror and embarrassment and wished all he had said was untrue. But she had to admit to herself that it wasn't.

She also wished he did not know her so well. They both realised in the same instant just how accurately he had analysed her feelings.

Sam and Peter had nearly reached them when two tears spilled from her eyes and slid down her cheeks.

She stared pleadingly at Ian, devastated

by the reality of her emotions and desperate that Sam should not discover it.

"Why don't you have a walk?" Ian murmured, rising to his feet. "I'll take care of it."

Jennifer did not need a second invitation. Instead, she turned and ran down the beach, her brain a jumble of confusion as she put as much distance between herself and the man who was the cause of her anxieties.

After a few minutes, she stopped, and sat down heavily in the sand. She clasped her arms around her knees and gazed out at the sea as it shimmered in the moonlight.

By the time Ian reached her a few minutes later, she almost had herself under control again, and was furious with herself for her irrational behaviour. Ian kneeled down behind her and wrapped his arms around her to hold her comfortingly back against him.

"I'm sorry, Jen, I didn't mean to upset you by saying all those things."

"I know that," she allowed, squeezing his arm. "I shouldn't be so touchy."

Ian's voice was full of concern.

"Sam's really special to you, isn't he?"

"I hardly know anything about him. I just know that when I'm with him, I feel different and it scares me."

"That idiot, Nigel, really knocked the stuffing out of you, Jen, I know that, but you can't shut yourself off like this," he told her, unknowingly repeating Sam's advice.

"I don't know if I'm ready to get involved with anyone again," she admitted, biting her lip. "Even if Sam was interested."

"You think he isn't?"

"We're just friends." Jennifer shrugged.

"Are you sure that's all he wants, to be friends?" Ian sounded sceptical. "From what little I've seen, I'd say he feels more for you than that."

"I don't know." Jennifer sighed. "I made it plain enough I wasn't interested in a relationship. He's accepted it so easily it makes me wonder if it was my imagination that there was ever anything else there at all. He treats me as a sister . . . just like Mark and Peter and you."

Ian rested his chin on the top of her head.

"Whatever is meant to happen, will happen. Give it time. You know where I am if you need a shoulder."

"Thanks Ian." She turned in his arms to kiss his cheek. "I'm sorry for being silly."

"Don't be daft! Shall we go back?" he added after a moment.

Jennifer shook her head.

"No, I'll stay here for a while if you don't mind. You go on."

"If you're sure. I must admit I've seen an attractive blonde who might be worth approaching."

Laughter bubbled up inside Jennifer.

"Ian! I swear you get worse."

Ian returned her laughter and tweaked her hair.

"Some would say I get better!" He

kissed her and stood up. "You're sure you'll be all right?"

"I'll be fine."

Jennifer watched him walk away, back towards the crowd that still mingled round the fire. From long experience she knew Ian would respect her confidence, and she did feel better for talking to him.

Perhaps to others their relationship was unusual, but she knew she would never have a better friend.

Jennifer sensed rather than heard Sam's approach. She glanced round and saw him strolling along the beach towards her.

He was wearing a pair of black cords and a pale blue shirt, and like her, his feet were bare. Without a word, he sat down beside her on the sand.

"I didn't know you were coming," Jennifer said at last, needing to break the silence that stretched between them.

"Last-minute decision," he explained as he leaned back on his hands. He glanced across and studied her. "Are you OK?"

"Yes, thanks. Fully recovered from the hectic week of the exhibition and getting back into some kind of normality again."

"That's not what I meant." He scolded her with mock reproach.

"Oh."

"When you ran off like that, I thought you were upset."

Jennifer fixed her gaze on the sea where it lapped at the sand.

"Ian was just teasing me and I took the bait," she excused.

"I see."

Jennifer doubted that he did but was grateful for the reprieve.

"What time do you want to leave?" Sam asked after a pause. He looked at her for a moment as if unsure what to say. "Ian's gone, you see."

She smiled into the darkness. She wasn't surprised. She had witnessed Ian in action before and even she had to admit he could be pretty irresistible!

"Blonde, was she?"

Sam frowned.

"No, a redhead. Do you mind?"

"Mind? Why should I?"

Sam's frown deepened as he watched her.

"I guess I made a mistake."

Unable to stop herself, Jennifer laughed.

"You don't think Ian and I — "

"Why not?" he protested, unamused at her reaction. "I didn't want to see you hurt, that's all."

"I'm sorry if you got the wrong idea. Thanks for thinking about me."

Jennifer stood up and went to paddle in the shallows. The water was surprisingly warm.

"You and Ian aren't . . . together?" Sam asked, following her.

"Gracious, no!"

Sam thrust his hands into his pockets and faced her.

"So what's the story then?"

"We were born within a couple of days of each other and our mothers, already friends, shared a room in hospital. We grew up together, went to the same schools, spent most of our time together right from when we were toddlers."

She tucked a stray wisp of hair behind her ear and smiled at him.

"We've been in all kinds of scrapes together, he watches over me, teases me mercilessly . . . he's the best friend I've ever had, and neither of us would want it any other way."

She discovered as they walked back towards the barbecue, the ripples lapping gentle at their feet, that Sam was down for the week-end.

★ ★ ★

On Saturday, he disappeared on a mysterious outing with Peter, and Jennifer spent the day in her studio, working on the portrait. She was annoyed, she admitted, then admonished herself.

She had only herself to blame for the

way things had turned out, and she was just too scared to trust her instincts and admit she had been wrong.

On Sunday, she took Sam to one of her favourite events of the Festival. It had not been official for a number of years, but her crowd of friends had so much fun, they had kept it going between them. There were already a large number of people milling about when they arrived, and she was lucky to find a place to park at the pub.

Jennifer spotted Ian in the company of a red-haired girl she knew by sight. He waved, took the girl's hand, and came across to join them.

"Sorry to ditch you the other night," he whispered in her ear as he hugged her. "Thought you'd understand."

"And I thought she was blonde!"

Ian pulled a face.

"Quiet. You'll get me a reputation!"

"You manage that well enough on your own," Jennifer teased with a laugh.

He tried to look hurt and failed.

"This is Clare," he said, drawing her forward. "Clare, my best friend, Jennifer, and Sam, a friend of the family." They shook hands and she tried to ignore Ian's provoking wink.

"We'd better go and find a good place," Ian continued. "We want to give our ducks a good start."

"Our what?" Sam questioned incredulously.

Ian laughed at the confused expression on Sam's face.

"Haven't you explained the seriousness and complexity of today's activities, Jen?"

"I was keeping it as a surprise."

"Shame on you," Ian chided. "He should have gone into training weeks ago."

"Would somebody tell me what's going on?" Sam asked.

Jennifer laughed at the mystified look on his face and went to the car to take two items from the boot. She walked back and handed Sam a plastic duck.

"I don't believe this!"

Ian grinned and ushered them ahead of him.

"Come along, gang, I feel success in my bones!"

At the appointed time, a flotilla of ducks was released by eager hands, and shouts of encouragement followed them on their journey downstream.

Some of the crowd walked along the riverbank, some went back to town by car. Sam and Jennifer stayed on foot and kept in line with the bobbing ducks.

Sam groaned when a couple of ducks were caught up in the reeds at a bend in the river.

All were marked with numbers underneath, but there was no way to identify individual ducks during the race.

"The first one to reach Arundel Bridge wins," Jennifer told him. "It won't be mine, not with my luck."

Sam smiled at her.

"What happens to yours?"

"Last year mine diverted off and

went down the mill stream, but I still insist it was sabotage!"

"Is the whole week like this?"

"No." She laughed. "This is just us being silly. There are various kinds of sporting events, exhibitions, things for the children, and of course, plays and concerts."

By the time they reached the bridge, it was clear that none of their ducks had won. Jennifer was not surprised. It was the taking part that was so much fun.

They got a lift back up the valley to where they had left the car and said their goodbyes to Ian and Clare.

Jennifer had been pleased to see Sam and Ian getting along so well. It meant a lot to her, and clearly they shared similar interests and a sense of humour.

"I like him," Ian whispered to her when he gave her a parting hug. "Don't let the chance go begging, Jen."

She smiled teasingly at him.

"I like Clare, too . . . how about

following your own advice?"

"Maybe I will — you never know."

His enigmatic reply surprised her. Ian getting serious? She hoped so, wished he would find someone to compliment his personality who could accommodate his free spirit. He had so much to offer — hopefully Clare would be that person.

"Fancy some lunch?" Sam suggested after the others had gone.

"Lovely. I'm famished!"

They sat at a table outside in the pub garden from where they had a good view of the river.

It was another glorious day.

Sam watched Jennifer with amusement as she tucked into her plate of roast beef and Yorkshire pudding with all the trimmings.

Jennifer noticed him looking and smiled.

"I missed breakfast . . . and the food here is great."

"I'm not complaining." He poured her another glass of red wine. "I suppose you are going to find room for dessert as well."

"I hope so! I may not move from here for a week, mind you!"

"I'll carry you back to the car." Sam laughed at her.

"Thanks. So what plans do you have for the near future? I was hoping . . . "

"I have a busy time coming up, what with the start of the season," he told her, before she could say anything else.

Jennifer held back a sigh of frustration and told herself she was relieved she had not made an idiot of herself and told him that she hoped they could spend some more time together.

Sam clearly thought of her in a platonic way . . . and a platonic way only. Jennifer hid her disappointment and smiled at him.

"You won't be down so much then? Peter will be sorry not to see you."

Sam glanced at her, the expression in his eyes difficult to read.

"Mmm," he murmured non-committally as he pushed his plate aside

342

and took a drink of his wine.

"So what do you have planned then?"

"The Charity Shield in a week or so, and I have a series of interviews to do. I'll be going to Manchester, Liverpool, Newcastle, Birmingham and London over the next few weeks, on top of the first of the match reports."

"Sounds hectic." And tiring, she thought, what with all the travel. "You can't get home much."

He folded his arms and leaned on the table.

"Not a lot. My flat in Nottingham is more of a base, especially during the season. It's reasonably central for the places I have to visit."

"You must get fed up with driving about."

"It can get a bit monotonous." He smiled. "But I love the job so it's worth it."

Jennifer was sorry when lunch was over and it was time to leave. More so when she discovered that Sam was

343

driving back that evening.

Back at the house, he had a chat with her father in the study, and Jennifer was intrigued to know what they were discussing. Not that it was her business, she added to herself.

"I'll keep in touch and let you know how things are going," her father promised him as the door opened and they stepped out.

Jennifer retreated into the living-room and hoped they had not seen her. An ache settled inside her when Sam glanced in and smiled.

"I'm just off," he said.

"Right." Jennifer heaved a sigh and followed him down the hall.

A wave of disappointment swamped her when all she received was a brief peck on the cheek by way of a parting gesture. Even that made her skin tingle. Her mother, Jennifer noted somewhat crossly, received an affectionate hug.

It was ironic, this talent she had to collect brothers, she mocked herself later that evening as she worked on

Sam's portrait. Knowing it was her own fault, that she had set the rules, did nothing to ease the ache of longing.

* * *

Jennifer felt flat and listless over the next two or three weeks. She forced herself to work, to keep her outlets supplied and to build up a stock of paintings. But it was Sam's portrait she worked on with the most love and attention.

It was finished by the beginning of September, and even Jennifer, normally critical of her own work, was thrilled with the result. Now all she had to do was present it to him.

With some detective work, she had discovered Sam would be in London on his birthday, and as luck would have it he rang to leave the number of his hotel for her father. He sounded rushed and tired, but his voice was wonderful to her ears.

"I've just finished the book," he told

her. "I just have to print it out and send it to my agent."

"That's great. Have you started the radio work yet?"

"Last week-end . . . I did a match report. I couldn't stop shaking, but it went OK." He paused and she heard him talking to someone in the background. "Listen, Jenny, I have to go. Pass on the number to your dad for me."

"I will. 'Bye."

She stared at the telephone for several moments, and knew all of a sudden what she would do. She had allowed her fears and past experience to hold her back from what she wanted, but not any more. It was time — time to take her biggest risk yet.

8

ON the morning of Sam's birthday, Jennifer carefully packed his portrait in her car and set off for London.

Like Sam with his match report, she couldn't stop shaking. She just hoped that the outcome of her journey into the unknown would be as successful as his. Her insides were knotted with nerves.

She had prepared well for her expedition, choosing her outfit with care, and even informing her parents she would be in Surrey until late that night delivering a painting ... an uncharacteristic white lie. It was important no-one spoil her surprise.

Having set off in buoyant mood, butterflies danced alarmingly as she neared her destination. Doubts set in. What if he laughed at her? But she loved him so much, she had to take the chance.

Even his voice made her tingle! She had listened to him on the radio just the day before, and the sound of it made her glow.

Not that she was interested in following the match. It was the feeling of being close to him that had held her attention.

It took a while to find a parking space near the hotel, and by the time Jennifer removed the picture, her courage was beginning to fail her. She took a deep breath, resolutely straightened her shoulders, and walked to the hotel. The journey only took five minutes but it seemed like an eternity to Jennifer.

In the reception area, she approached the desk and smiled at the young man on duty.

"Hello, can you tell me if Mr Harper is in, please?"

The clerk smiled back.

"I'll check for you." He moved to the rear of the alcove, checked the register and dialled a number on his phone. He stepped back to her after a moment. "I'm sorry, there is no reply from his room. Can I take a message? I'll see he gets it on his return."

"No, thank you," Jennifer replied, trying to hide her initial disappointment. "I'll wait for him."

"You could check the lounge."

Jennifer thanked him again and walked across the foyer in the direction he had pointed. A glance round the room told her Sam was not there. After her initial excitement, she now felt deflated, and had no idea how long she would have to wait.

She chose a comfortable chair by the door where she could see the hotel entrance and the reception desk.

The time dragged with painful slowness. The clock in the corner chimed every quarter hour and after hearing it four times, Jennifer decided she was an emotional wreck.

She walked across to the reception desk to discover there had been a change in shift and two women were now on duty.

"Can I help you?" one asked.

"I'm meeting someone." Jennifer smiled. "Could I have a cup of tea while I'm waiting?"

"Of course. I'll have it brought through to you."

She returned to her vigil, and continued to watch the entrance like a hawk. When her tea arrived, she paid the waiter and poured out a cup of the strong brew. She needed it as the next half hour or so still proved fruitless. Jennifer was beginning to wonder if her trip had been such a good idea after all.

But just then she noticed a woman arriving with a small child in tow. They walked across to the desk, and Jennifer found herself admiring the woman's style and poise, her perfectly tailored outfit, her dark, exotic looks.

As the woman spoke to the clerk at the desk, the little girl, a carbon copy of her mother and who Jennifer guessed was about three, turned in her direction and smiled. Jennifer smiled back, liking her on sight.

The woman took a key and turned towards the lifts, and Jennifer shifted her attention once more to the entrance. Then, the receptionist's voice held her rigid.

"Mrs Harper, just a moment please. I have a message for you from your husband."

The woman returned to the desk and accepted the envelope offered to her with a smile.

It had to be a coincidence, Jennifer assured herself. Harper was not an uncommon name, and . . . at that moment, she watched as Sam walked into the foyer.

The little girl shrieked with excitement, freed herself from her mother and ran across the lobby into Sam's arms.

Jennifer sat frozen with shock.

"How's my favourite girl?" Sam asked as he picked the child up and kissed her.

"OK. Mummy and I have bought you a present," she told him proudly.

Sam tousled her hair.

"That's very thoughtful. I'm sure I shall love it."

Jennifer watched as he put down the little girl and walked across to where the woman waited. He kissed her briefly and they moved off to the lifts.

It was an age before she could move. She was stunned. Her mind refused to function.

Thank goodness he had not seen her, but . . . She had to leave, had to get away before he came down again.

In a daze, Jennifer gathered up her bag and the portrait and returned to her car, her legs like jelly. She sat behind the wheel, her hands clenched, the knuckles white, feeling numb inside. As if she were acting on automatic pilot, she switched on the ignition and pulled jerkily away from the kerb.

As soon as Jennifer left the suburbs, she pulled off the road and into a layby.

She was shocked to realise she did not remember how she arrived there. She certainly had no recollection of driving. And it was all because of Sam . . .

Jennifer squeezed her eyes shut to try to stem the scalding rush of tears, but she could not. She buried her face in her hands as sobs racked her body.

How could this have happened to her a second time? She had been deceived. Sam had been playing with her, amusing himself at her expense, when all the time he had a wife and child tucked safely away in the background.

How could she have thought a man like him would be interested in her? Once bitten, twice shy. She should have heeded the warning. How could she have been so stupid?

★ ★ ★

As the light began to fade, she tried to pull herself together. She could not sit here all night. Nor could she face the prospect of going home.

The only alternative was to stay at Ian's until she could think rationally enough to decide how to try and put the pieces of her life back together again.

She started the engine and pulled out of the layby, heading slowly home. On the way to Ian's, she stopped at a call box to phone her mother, trying to sound as normal as she could as she offered an excuse for her continued absence. More lies, she chastised herself guiltily, as she drove back to Arundel.

As she parked outside Ian's building, she could see that his flat was in darkness. She groaned and leaned back in her seat. Perhaps he was in his darkroom? Just in case, she tried his bell, but there was no answer. Defeated, she returned to the car to wait.

Jennifer tried desperately not to think about the whole desperate situation, but her mind cruelly insisted on replaying the events of the afternoon.

Tears pricked her eyes once more as she saw Sam's face, his smile, the way he greeted his little girl . . . his wife.

She banged her fists against the steering wheel, furious with Sam for his duplicity, furious with herself for being so gullible.

She didn't want to feel sorry for herself, but she felt wretched . . . more lost and alone than ever in her life. She wanted nothing more than to crawl into a hole and never face the world ever again.

What was the point of anything if she did not have Sam to share it with? A sob escaped from her. How could he do this to her . . . ?

A flash of headlights alerted her to the arrival of a car. In the rearview mirror, she saw Ian get out. Wiping her face, she reached for her bag as he walked towards her and tapped on the driver's window.

"Jen?"

She opened the door and stepped

out, only to find that her whole body was shaking. Fresh tears welled up, beyond her control. Ian sighed sympathetically and wrapped his arms around her.

"I'm here, Jen," he soothed as he led her towards the door. "Let's get you inside."

He sat her on the ancient settee in his sitting-room then he went to the kitchen, poured a large brandy and gently placed it in her hand.

"Drink this."

Her fingers shook as she tried to hold the glass steady, but she raised it to her lips and took a sip.

Ian sat beside her and she cuddled up against him, comforted by his unquestioning affection and under-standing. She rested her head against his shoulder.

"Tell me what's happened," he murmured against her hair.

Jennifer sniffed and took another sip, coughing slightly as the amber liquid left a fiery trail down her throat.

"I've been so stupid."

"Take your time. Just start at the beginning."

"I've been painting a portrait of Sam," she told him in a shaky voice. "Today is his birthday. I wanted to surprise him, wanted to tell him . . . "

The thought of it was enough to make her shake again.

"You went to see him?" Ian prompted.

"Yes." She sniffed. "At his hotel."

"Go on." Ian stroked her hair.

"It was awful, Ian. I can't believe I could have been so gullible. I started to trust him, I thought . . . Oh, this is so difficult to say . . . The thing is, he's married," she finished in a hoarse whisper.

"He's what?" Ian drew away to look at her, his expression incredulous. "You're sure?"

"I saw him, with her — Mrs Harper the receptionist called her. There was . . . they have a little girl."

Ian muttered something that Jennifer didn't quite catch and tightened his hold around her shoulders.

"Did you manage to talk to him?"

"No. I didn't want him to see me. I don't ever want to see him again." Hot, salty tears slid down her cheeks. "Ian, what am I going to do? I really love . . ." She hesitated and corrected herself. "Loved him."

"Does your family know where you are?"

She shook her head.

"I told them I was delivering a painting in Surrey. I rang Mum, she thinks I'm still there. They don't know about Sam and I don't want them to, please, Ian."

"They won't hear anything from me."

"I know I shouldn't have lied to her but I couldn't face the thought of going home, not like this. Then I thought of you."

"I'm glad you did." Ian stood up and helped her to her feet. "I think you should try to get some sleep. At least if you get some rest it might be easier to try to work out what to do in the morning."

She did not resist when he ushered her through to his bedroom. After slipping off her dress, she snuggled down between the sheets, tired and emotionally drained. Ian came back to check on her, holding her hand until she drifted off into a restless sleep.

★ ★ ★

It was the light that woke her. A shaft of sunlight peeped through the curtains and traced a path across the pillow.

Jennifer sat up with a shock. It took a moment for her to remember where she was, what had happened, then she subsided with a groan. Sam! A knife twisted in her heart.

Listlessly, she slipped from the bed, pulled on her dress and went to the bathroom. She studied her face in the mirror and sighed. Her eyes were dull, her complexion paper-white.

After a wash she felt marginally more

human and went to find Ian.

A pillow and folded blanket were on the settee and the aroma of coffee drifted from the kitchen. She found him sitting at the table studying photographs.

He looked up when she walked in.

"'Morning."

"I know, I look a mess."

"I didn't say a thing."

Ian poured her coffee, but Jennifer refused his offer of food. She could not have forced anything past the restriction in her throat.

"Why aren't you at work?"

"I took the day off. I didn't want to leave you." He looked at her with a frown. "You know you can stay here as long as you like, but you are going to have to let your family know where you are and face them sometime, even if you don't tell them about Sam."

The sound of his name was like a physical pain.

"I know." She nodded her head but

she did not want to think about it. Not yet.

Jennifer finally allowed Ian to take her home that afternoon while the house was empty and she could spend a while on her own to have a bath and restore some composure.

"Whenever you need me, I'm here for you, Jen," Ian assured her as he left.

"I don't know what I'd do without you." She hugged him tight.

Despite her fears that her inner pain would show more obviously on the outside, Jennifer managed to present a normal front for the family that evening. Her mother was excited by a postcard from Europe from Mark saying he would be home at the end of the following week, and Jennifer was thankful not to be the centre of attention.

One day followed another with painful regularity. She spent most of her time in her studio, hardly eating, frightened to go to bed in case she dreamed of Sam. Her mother was suspicious but she had managed to deflect her attention . . . so far.

It was Ian who helped to keep Jennifer sane. She did not think she could have coped without his support and patient understanding.

* * *

One afternoon, more than a week after her nightmare trip to London, she left her studio, seeing anger and confusion in her brush strokes, and went to make tea. She was startled to find her mother in the kitchen, home early from work.

"I'm glad you've come down, Jennifer, I want to talk to you."

Jennifer poured herself a cup of tea and sat down, tracing a finger around the rim of her cup.

"I want to know what's wrong," her mother demanded. "Something has happened to make you unhappy. You've lost weight and I've never seen you looking so tired. I want to help, please let me."

"I'm not ready to talk about it. Try to understand. It's something I have to work out for myself."

"But — "

"Please, Mum." Jennifer clenched her fists. "I know you care. I'm sorry, but I need time."

Ann Wilson looked at her daughter for a long moment.

"All right, if that's what you want. But when you want to talk, I'm here to listen."

"Thank you."

★ ★ ★

The morning post brought a letter for Peter from Sam and two tickets for a football match for him and his friend, John. Peter was ecstatic, but when he started to read the letter out loud, Jennifer couldn't bear to stay and listen to his news.

She lowered her gaze from her

mother's probing stare and excused herself, scurrying to the privacy of her studio.

This was ridiculous. She could not allow Sam's deception to ruin her life, no matter how much it hurt. And it did hurt . . . more than she could have ever imagined.

Somehow, for her own sanity, she had to find a way to block him from her consciousness and get on with her life. She couldn't just stand there and let yet another man walk all over her.

In a more determined frame of mind, she went downstairs at lunchtime and forced herself to eat some toast. When the phone rang, she was startled, and spilled her coffee.

Tearing off a strip of kitchen towel to mop it up with one hand, she reached for the receiver with the other.

"Hello?"

"Jenny, it's Sam. How are you?"

The breath left her in a strangled gasp and she sat down on a chair, her mind numb.

"Are you still there?"

"Yes," she mumbled, finding her voice.

"You're a difficult person to talk to these days," he teased and she could hear the smile in his voice. It brought a lump to her throat. "I've been hoping to catch you. I wanted to tell you my news in person."

"Listen, Sam," she cut in, her own voice cool as she gathered her scattered wits. "I'm just on my way out to an appointment."

There was a pause and his tone was more wary when he spoke.

"Jenny, is anything wrong?"

"Why should there be?" she parried, regretting the chilly tone she was unable to disguise.

"Jenny — "

"I'm already late," she informed him coldly. "I have to go."

"Wait! Your mother is expecting me, tell her I'll be there by five. Jenny . . . " He paused again. "I'll see you then, we can — "

"Goodbye, Sam."

Jennifer closed her eyes and put the phone down on him. She was shaking. How could she face him?

Listening to that voice on the phone was enough to turn her into a nervous wreck. And he was coming here — today.

9

"**Y**OU look awful," Ian told Jennifer when he walked into his flat at six that evening. He arrived in the kitchen, saw she had laid the table and was cooking, and made a face. "Is it safe to eat?"

"Thanks very much for your kind compliments."

He poured himself a glass of orange juice and leaned against the counter, watching her.

"Your mum called in, wanted to know if I knew what was the matter with you."

"Oh." Jennifer threw him a startled glance.

"Don't look so worried, I didn't say anything." He frowned as he looked her over. "Looking at you, I can see why she's worried."

Jennifer refrained from comment and

dished up the spaghetti bolognese she had prepared. She put a jug of water and two glasses on the table, then sat down and served a plateful to Ian.

He took a wary taste and his eyebrows lifted.

"Hey, it's not bad!"

Jennifer returned his smile but she could not muster up much sense of humour. All she could think of was Sam.

He would be at the house now, and after the way she spoke to him on the phone, he must realise she was avoiding him. Would he say anything to her mother?

After his phone call, her only thought had been to escape. She despised herself for running away, but what else could she do? She shuddered at the thought. That would be impossible.

Instead, she had written a note to her mother to say she had received an invitation from Ian and would be away for a day or two. Then, feeling guilty, she had added a PS in a different pen, and hoped her mother would be duped into believing Sam's message had arrived some time afterwards.

"Do you want to tell me what's going on?"

Jennifer started at the sound of Ian's voice, colour in her cheeks as she looked up at him.

"Sam's coming down this evening, I just couldn't . . . "

"I don't mind being used as a scapegoat, Jen," he told her gently when her voice trailed off, "but are you sure you're doing the right thing?"

"It was all I could think of on the spur of the moment. Just hearing him on the phone threw me into a panic. I had to get away and you were the person I wanted to see."

Ian twisted some spaghetti on his fork.

"You can't run away for ever, you know. Sooner or later you are going to have to face him and deal with this. Are you going to tell your family? Do you expect them to stop seeing him?"

"No . . . on both counts." How could she explain what a first-class idiot she had been and imagine they would somehow banish Sam from their lives. No, the problem was hers and hers alone.

"So what are you going to do?" Ian persisted. "You can't just dash out of the house every time he threatens a visit."

"I know. It was just so sudden." Jennifer sighed. "It's too soon. Ian, I don't know what to do."

To her relief, he let the subject drop for the time being. She knew she would have to learn to control her outward emotions, that she must find a way to meet Sam and present a cool, polite outward façade. But how?

How could she love him and hate him at one and the same time? To hear his voice was bad enough. To see him may be her undoing. Despite all her anguish and soul-searching, she was no nearer a solution to her problem.

Ian took her out that evening to

see a comedy at a local cinema. She enjoyed herself, but felt guilty as she was suspicious he had postponed a date with Clare so he could keep her company.

He refused to discuss it, however, and although Jennifer did not press the point, she vowed to make sure it did not happen again.

Back at his flat, they had a friendly argument about who would sleep where, and Jennifer finally gave in and saw Ian relegated to the uncomfortable settee once more.

It took her ages to sleep. Every time she closed her eyes, she had an image of Sam in her mind, tormenting her, mocking her. And it wouldn't go away . . .

* * *

"Jen? Jen, are you awake?"

"Mmm?"

The door opened and Ian came in, giving her shoulder a shake.

"I have to go to work. I've left coffee in the pot, and I've made you some breakfast. Make sure you eat it."

Jennifer stirred when Ian left. She washed and dressed and went through to his tiny kitchen. She sipped the coffee and picked guiltily at the food he had prepared for her, but her stomach protested. She just wasn't hungry.

After a half-hearted glance through the paper, she turned her attention to deciding on her plans for the day.

She was hampered by not knowing the duration of Sam's visit. Despite her resolutions of the previous evening to confront the situation, her courage had waned in the clear light of day.

When the telephone rang, she answered it, expecting it to be Ian checking up on her.

"Hello," she greeted, a smile in her voice.

"It's me, Jen," her mother informed, startling her. "I'm at work, but I promised your father I would ring."

"What is it?" Jennifer sat down feeling wary.

"One of his clients has bought that lovely old country house on the other side of town. You know the one, down the lane where the Rogers used to live?"

"I know it," she confirmed. It was a beautiful house in a magnificent position and it had only been on the market a short time.

"Your father is handling the legal affairs. The new owner has seen your work and wants you to paint a series of pictures that will compliment the house and the setting. What do you think?"

"If it's landscapes they want I'd be interested," she allowed, feeling the glow of excitement inside. "I'll get in touch and we can discuss it."

"Excellent," her mother responded with enthusiasm. "I don't know what your plans are, but I said I would ask you to call round today."

Jennifer had no time to protest.

"Any time after eleven, I was told.

It seems too good an opportunity to miss, dear."

"Yes. Yes, it does."

"Right then. I'll have to go. I'm taking a client out to view properties this morning. I hope all goes well."

"Thanks, Mum. You, too."

Jennifer hung up, puzzled by her mother's breezy attitude. She had sounded so hail and hearty, and no mention had been made of her absence. Perhaps she was being too touchy, Jennifer pondered.

There had been no mention of Sam, either. Had he already left? Maybe he had never arrived after all.

She shrugged Sam from her mind with dogged determination and set herself to concentrate on the task in hand.

"Blast," she muttered as she gathered up her bag and her materials. She had completely forgotten to ask her mother these clients' names.

She tried to phone back, but her mother had already left, and she knew that her father would be in court all day.

Never mind, if her visit was expected, she would muddle over the introductions somehow.

It was almost noon when she turned down the drive of the house. Her gaze ran over the old, Sussex-style house, built of flint with brick quoins, with appreciation.

It had a low-pitched roof of slate, with two flint chimney stacks. Ivy climbed haphazardly over the front of the house and around the north-facing, solid front door.

Jennifer crossed the gravelled drive. A walled garden was hidden from her sight, but she knew from a past visit to the house that the view over the river valley to the south was exceptional. As she reached the house, she discovered the front door was ajar and she peeped inside to view the entrance hall, panelled with oak.

She tried the bell-pull but nothing happened. Jennifer stepped inside the surprisingly spacious hall and found herself at the foot of a curving staircase.

"Hello? Is anyone there?"

When there was no reply, she moved towards an open door that led off the hall.

She stepped into a large, airy living-room, and on impulse she walked across to the picture windows to find that the view was even more spectacular than she had remembered.

Away at the foot of the valley, the coil of the river glinted silver in the sunshine.

She heard the door close behind her and swung round, guilty at having intruded into someone else's house, and was unprepared for the sight that met her eyes.

10

FOR one awful moment, as her shocked gaze registered Sam leaning back against the door, Jennifer thought she would faint. Her legs turned to jelly, and she put out a trembling hand to clutch the back of a chintz-covered chair in an effort to steady herself.

Dressed in jeans and a green shirt, he looked as incredibly handsome as ever. Jennifer began to shake. As he straightened up and started to cross the room towards her, Jennifer jumped like a startled rabbit, and hastily put the width of a large, mahogany table between them. The smile left Sam's face as he stared at her in astonishment.

"What on earth have you done to yourself?"

It's you, she wanted to cry, you've

done this to me. Instead, she looked at him, speechless, her dull eyes wide with horror at her predicament.

"Jenny?"

She cleared her throat and cursed the waver in her voice she was unable to control.

"What are you doing here?"

"I own the house," he told her with a puzzled frown. "Didn't your mother tell you?"

Jennifer shook her head, stunned by the knowledge that her mother had tricked her into going, knowing who owned the house.

Why had she done it? She had made Jennifer look like an idiot. It was too terrible for words.

"Your family said they were worried about you," Sam informed her, concern in his voice. "I can understand why. Are you ill?"

"I'm quite well, thank you," she responded, her voice stiff. "I came to say I am unable to undertake the commission."

"Excuse me?" Sam looked perplexed.

"The paintings," she snapped, tension playing on her nerves. "I can't do them."

"I never mentioned any paintings. I simply suggested you might like to see the house."

She could hear the edge of annoyance in Sam's voice as he started to move around the table towards her. She glanced over at the door and stepped towards it. His eyes narrowed. Jennifer cursed her mother for landing her in this situation.

"I'll be going then," she told him coldly.

Sam closed off her line of retreat.

"You've only just arrived. Don't you want to look round?"

"No."

"Jenny, what is it?"

"Nothing." She evaded the hand he reached out to her, unsettled by the determination and vexation in his eyes. "I have things to do."

"I want to talk to you, and I

especially want to know why you have been avoiding me."

"I don't have time." She stared at the wall.

"Don't treat me like an idiot," Sam snapped with irritation, his patience stretched to the limit. "What's going on?"

"Nothing."

Resentment curled inside her, festering. She clenched her hands into fists, and watched him from beneath her lashes as he clearly battled with his temper.

"Come with me," he said, his voice more controlled. "I want to show you something. Please."

Short of making a dash for the door, Jennifer did not see how she could avoid him. Besides, he was faster and stronger than she was, and she had never seen him in such a cross, determined mood. Perhaps if she did as he asked, and saw whatever it was, she would find the opportunity to make her escape.

"All right," she finally agreed with bad grace.

With deep reluctance, she followed as he led the way upstairs and along a corridor. She refused to glance in any of the rooms. She did not want to see the house he would share with his family.

The very thought of it made tears prick the back of her eyes, but she forced them away. She would not allow herself to break down in front of him.

At the end of the passage, he opened a door into a large room that Jennifer guessed was above the garage.

It was bare of furniture, the walls finished in cream. Sam crossed the room and pulled up the blinds to allow a perfect north light to fill the room.

"As soon as I saw it, I thought it would make a wonderful studio," Sam informed her with a return of a smile.

Jennifer felt the blood drain from her face as she stared at him. She tried to imagine the elegant woman in the

London hotel with ink on her fingers and paint on her clothes, and couldn't. She bit back a fresh rush of tears and forced herself to speak.

"Does your wife paint?"

"I haven't asked her yet."

Jennifer felt as if she had been poleaxed. The swine had not even denied it, had made no attempt to cover his treachery.

How could he be so cruel? Had he no idea what this was doing to her? It had been the worst thing he could have shown her . . .

Knowing she could not contain her tears a moment longer, Jennifer turned and ran from the room, back along the corridor and down the staircase.

Behind her, she heard Sam call her name, heard his footsteps as he came after her, but she did not slow her flight. She had to get away from him.

In a panic, she fumbled with the keys of her car, and dropped them on the gravel. Blinded by hot tears, she searched for them in vain.

Sam's hands closed on her shoulders. She fought, struggled desperately to free herself from him, lashing out wildly.

"Jenny, stop it." Sam caught her flailing hands. "Jenny — "

"I have to go. Leave me alone. Just leave me alone . . . " she finished, her voice choking to a halt on a sob.

"You're not going anywhere in this state."

Jennifer tried to resist as he took her back inside the house but he was too strong.

She found herself seated on the settee in his living-room, and as Sam sat down beside her, she shook off his hands and edged away, angry with herself that his touch could still stir her blood.

"Tell me what's the matter!"

She wiped her eyes with the back of her hand, refusing the tissue he held out for her. She set her face mutinously.

There was no way she was going to admit anything to him! When she tried to get up, Sam grasped her wrist and forced her back down beside him. Jennifer flashed him a look of pure hatred.

"Don't touch me," she spat.

Sam relaxed his hold, his eyes troubled.

"Jenny, I care about you, we all do. I want to help you."

"I don't need any help, especially not yours," she finally stormed, unable to contain her pain and resentment. "You've done more than enough already. I trusted you and you lied to me. You told me to tell you, and now I have. I hate you."

"What in the world are you talking about?"

"Don't pretend you don't know."

"I don't. What am I supposed to have done, Jenny? I thought we were friends," he finished, hurt lacing his voice.

"You are not my friend. You don't care about me at all." Against her better judgement, she glanced at him and saw the pain on his face. "I saw you. Watched you with my own eyes."

"Saw what?" Sam's worried frown deepened.

"You. You with your wife and child," she shouted at him, struggling to be free and put some distance between them. He refused to release her.

"Jenny, I have never been married and I don't have any children," he told her quietly.

"But I saw you . . . "

"Tell me what happened."

Jennifer did, and found that once she began, she couldn't stop. She explained about the portrait, her surprise trip to London, the scene she had witnessed . . . the words were tripping over each other as she poured out her hurt and confusion.

By the time she had finished, Sam had wrapped his arms around her and she did not have the strength or the will to resist. He was so warm and comforting. As her tears dried, she sniffed, then suddenly realised he was chuckling.

"Don't you dare laugh at me," she accused, so angry she could hit him. Even now he wasn't taking her seriously.

"I'm sorry." He attempted to wipe the smile from his face. "Barbara is married to my brother, David, and Elaine is their daughter. They had just flown back from Gibraltar after joining him for leave."

"Well, how I was supposed to know that?"

"You could have asked me. Better yet, you could have trusted me."

Jennifer felt chastened at the gentle censure in his tone.

"After what happened with Nigel, when I saw you, I assumed the worst. I asked you once if you were married and you said I should find out for myself. I thought I had."

Sam started to shake his head.

"I said that because I was angry with you for thinking so little of me that I would use you like that while being married to someone else," he explained. "My intention was to make you trust me."

"But upstairs, the studio, you implied you had a wife and had not asked her about painting," Jennifer accused.

Sam smiled again.

"No I didn't, you misunderstood. I meant that I had not asked the lady in question to marry me."

Jennifer's heart flipped over as she looked at him. Sam brushed some strands of hair back from her face.

Disbelief gripped her. She stood up and walked across to the windows to gaze out at the view as she tried to compose her thoughts. Sam's words were finally beginning to make sense to her.

"You want to marry me?" she asked in amazement as she turned to face him. "Why? You haven't been anything but casually friendly for weeks."

"That was what you wanted, not me," Sam reminded her.

"But . . . "

"I was trying to give you space and hoping you wouldn't take too long to discover you couldn't live without me." He crossed the room and slipped his arms around her waist. "Jenny, I know this has all happened so quickly, and it's not surprising you were wary. I'm not proclaiming to be a saint, but there was no-one special in my life when I met you, and there hasn't been anybody but you since."

She linked her arms around his neck and leaned against him.

"I've been so miserable," she whispered.

He tipped her chin up with one finger and bent to kiss her. It started as a gesture of reassurance, but rapidly deepened into something more.

Jennifer tightened her hold on him, afraid to let him go. Being in his arms felt like coming home. When Sam put her away from him, she protested. He smiled in amusement at her grumpy complaint as he led her to the kitchen and pulled out a chair for her.

"Sit."

"I'm not a dog," she chided, smiling at his command.

Sam's smile widened to a grin.

"I know — you aren't properly trained!"

"Why, you — "

"Now, now, I've warned you about language before." He teased her as he took some cold meat and salad from the fridge and set a plate before her. "You need feeding up."

"If I do as I'm told, do I earn a reward?"

Sam's eyes crinkled at the corners as he returned her grin.

"I expect I'll think of something!"

As Jennifer ate her meal, her appetite returning, Sam spoke of his news.

"I've been offered a job fronting a new football programme on TV," he told her. "It would still mean some travelling to matches and that kind of thing, and I can still have time to write the other biographies lined up . . . What do you think?"

"I think it's terrific. If it's what you want to do, go for it."

"What I want is a proper home, a family . . . with you."

"Oh, Sam." Jennifer slid from her seat and went round the table to wriggle on to his lap. "Are you sure I'm not dreaming? Ouch!" she complained when he gave her a playful pinch.

"You aren't dreaming!" He laughed at her.

She buried her face against him.

"I'm sorry I've been so stupid. Ian said — "

"Ah, yes, Ian."

Jennifer looked at him, anxious about the edge in his tone.

"You do like him, don't you?"

"Yes, I do. But I can't begin to tell you how jealous I was when he arrived back from holiday." He slanted a wry glance at her. "You did that on purpose, didn't you? I've never seen you so enthusiastic about a man before."

"No, of course I didn't! I honestly never thought how you would view my relationship with Ian. Besides, by then I didn't think you were really interested in me anyway."

"What?"

She smiled at the incredulity in his voice.

"I told you I was stupid."

"About Ian. I know your friendship is special and I don't want anything to change that," Sam assured her quietly. "I was just unsure how you felt about me and was envious of your closeness, his place in your affections."

"You have first place in my affections," she assured him and added in a whisper, "I love you, Sam."

His fingers sank into her hair.

"Jenny, the first time I saw you, all beautiful and prickly and spoiling for a fight, it was like a bolt from the blue. I never stood a chance."

"I was a bit prickly, wasn't I?"

Sam smiled, his eyes darkening as he looked at her.

"Before I get sidetracked, I think I'd better take you home and put your mother out of her misery," he told her huskily as he set her on her feet and stood up, brushing some hair out of Jennifer's face.

"Then what?" Jennifer asked as she snuggled against him.

"I can't believe you painted a portrait of me. I'd love to see it." He looked down at her with suspicious amusement. "Or do I? You haven't added devil's horns or been throwing darts at it, have you?"

"The thought never crossed my mind!" Jennifer replied slyly.

Sam pulled her closer and tipped her face up for his kiss. She tightened her hold on him. Only he could make her feel like this. When he drew back, his eyes were dark, his smile rueful.

"I said I wasn't going to get sidetracked . . ."

"Sam — "

"Listen, Jenny. We'll take this one step at a time. I don't want to rush you, I want you to be sure this is what you want. I — "

Jennifer placed her fingers against his lips silencing his words.

"Sam, be quiet," she ordered softly. "I like being sidetracked, and you are what I want." Before he could argue, she pulled his mouth back to hers.

THE END

A YOUNG MAN'S FANCY
Nancy Bell

Six people get together for reasons of their own, and the result is one of misunderstanding, suspicion and mounting tension.

THE WISDOM OF LOVE
Janey Blair

Barbie meets Louis and receives flattering proposals, but her reawakened affection for Jonah develops into an overwhelming passion.

MIRAGE IN THE MOONLIGHT
Mandy Brown

En route to an island to be secretary to a multi-millionaire, Heather's stubborn loyalty to her former flatmate plunges her into a grim hazard.